Dead in t

A Heavenly Highland Inn Cozy Mystery

Cindy Bell

Copyright © 2013 Cindy Bell
All rights reserved.

All rights reserved. No part of this publication may be reproduced or transmitted in any form or by any means, electronic or mechanical, including photocopy, recording, or any information storage or retrieval system, without permission in writing from the publisher.

This is a work of fiction. The characters, incidents and locations portrayed in this book and the names herein are fictitious. Any similarity to or identification with the locations, names, characters or history of any person, product or entity is entirely coincidental and unintentional.

All trademarks and brands referred to in this book are for illustrative purposes only, are the property of their respective owners and not affiliated with this publication in any way. Any trademarks are being used without permission, and the publication of the trademark is not authorized by, associated with or sponsored by the trademark owner.

ISBN-13: 978-1493744121

ISBN-10: 1493744127

More Cozy Mysteries by Cindy Bell

Bekki the Beautician Cozy Mysteries

Hairspray and Homicide

A Dyed Blonde and a Dead Body

Mascara and Murder

Pageant and Poison

Heavenly Highland Inn Cozy Mysteries

Murdering the Roses

Table of Contents

CHAPTER ONE 1

CHAPTER TWO 17

CHAPTER THREE 43

CHAPTER FOUR..63

CHAPTER FIVE..84

CHAPTER SIX... 105

CHAPTER SEVEN 118

CHAPTER EIGHT 136

Chapter One

Sarah had turned as white as a sheet. She could not believe this was happening. Her younger sister, Vicky, noticed Sarah's shocked expression as she walked up to the front desk of the Heavenly Highland Inn.

"Sarah? What's wrong?" Vicky asked as her features creased into a concerned frown.

"You will not believe it," Sarah said with absolute certainty, her lips tensing around each word to emphasize just how astounding her news would be. Vicky was drawn in by the dramatic dangling of information.

"Well, I can't," she laughed quietly as she leaned against the reception desk. "If you don't tell me what it is."

Sarah drew a deep breath and then glanced at the phone as if she was still trying to decide whether she had heard the news correctly. When she looked back at Vicky she blurted out her words. "Seth and Trinie want to get married here!" she squealed and clapped her hands as if she was a teenage girl again. Vicky might have laughed at this if she wasn't too busy squealing and clapping her hands in the same way. She immediately recognized the names of one of the most famous celebrity couples.

Sarah was older than Vicky by five years but in many ways it seemed like a lifetime. Vicky was still at a stage in her life where she wanted to have fun and was a much more spontaneous and rebellious person by nature. Sarah was more serious and always wanted to be in control. That was why she was the manager and in charge of the day to day business of the grand, old Heavenly Highland Inn, while Vicky took charge of the party planning. This suited both sisters just fine, as Sarah enjoyed the managerial duties, while Vicky had a knack for creating the perfect event for their guests, no matter what the occasion

"The Seth and Trinie?" a shrill voice inquired from behind them, announcing the presence of Aunt Ida. Vicky turned with shining eyes to see her Aunt Ida looking as if she might simply tip over from the news. Aunt Ida wrung her hands together in excited anticipation. "Is it true? Is it?" she asked eagerly as she joined her young nieces at the desk. She had taken a motherly role in their lives after Vicky and Sarah's parents had met an unexpected demise in a tragic car accident. Although she was not the most nurturing soul, she did love her nieces fiercely, and would do anything for either of them.

She was one of the most eccentric women that Vicky had ever met and she showed it from the colorful scarf she had tied around her neck, to the blazing red high heels she had her feet tucked into. She was always wearing the latest, and loudest fashions. Today she was adorned in a silk suit that looked a bit like an impressionist painting with every bright color tossed onto one piece of material. The scarf tied around her neck matched the silk sash tied around her waist. She looked stunning, and there was really no way to tell from her features exactly what her age might be. She always had a youthful glow, and would challenge anyone to guess the year she was born. Sarah and Vicky were fairly certain they knew the actual answer, that Aunt Ida was in her sixties, but she could easily fool anyone into believing she had just graced the forties with her presence.

Vicky grabbed her aunt gently by the elbow to help steady her before she nodded with a grin accompanying her words. "Yes, it's true. The Seth and Trinie, they're coming here to get married!"

Aunt Ida did sway a little in Vicky's steady grasp but she managed to stay on her feet.

"Well, that is just amazing!" she gushed, her cheeks filling with color. "I knew that the tennis season had just finished up and Seth had taken some time off, and that Trinie had just finished that movie, but I had no idea they were planning to get married!"

"That's because no one is supposed to know," Sarah said sternly as she looked at her aunt with a mixture of affection and warning. "We need to keep this to ourselves until we're given the green light to share the information with others."

"Well, how can we do that?" Aunt Ida whined quietly as she looked at the two girls. "Weddings take months to plan! Are we supposed to keep this secret for months? I don't know if I can do that," she said with absolute honesty.

"Not this one," Sarah said with a grimace as she looked at Vicky with a sense of foreboding in her eyes. "That's the other part of the news," she said hesitantly.

"What?" Vicky asked with growing anxiety as she saw the tell tale crease in her sister's forehead that indicated she was trying really hard to stay calm.

"It's a last minute decision because the filming for Trinie's new movie was brought forward and they are going to be away filming for months so they want to get married this weekend!" she announced all at once and then cringed, waiting for the onslaught of fury and panic.

Vicky felt every breath leave her body at once. She had certainly planned plenty of weddings in a relatively short time frame, but never a celebrity wedding! The wealthy usually had so many demands and expectations about their big day that Vicky would spend hours a day for months leading up to the wedding making sure everything was perfect.

"Oh, this is terrible," Sarah groaned and rubbed her forehead as she expected Vicky's reaction to be one of panic.

"It's not terrible," Vicky insisted surprisingly, her words spoken along with a bright smile. "We can make it happen," she snapped her fingers together and nodded with confidence.

"But, what if we can't?" Sarah asked and looked from her aunt to her sister. "What if it's a disaster and then the entire world hears what a terrible inn we run? We'll be finished," her shoulders slumped at the idea. "Having Seth and Trinie get married here could be like winning the lottery, or getting hit with a curse," she frowned.

Vicky rolled her eyes at her sister's anticipation of the negative. "Don't worry about it, I can handle it," Vicky assured her cheerfully. "This is an amazing opportunity," she said with a smile. "I'm going to take care of everything."

This was an opportunity they could not pass up because not only was it a high profile wedding but the wedding season had been a bit dismal. This was very unusual for one of the most popular and sought after wedding destinations. Unfortunately, bad weather and a troubled economy had caused business to be much slower than usual. Sarah had been on edge, waiting for some of the advertising she had done to pay off. They did have plenty of vacation stays booked, but the real money maker for the inn was the wedding season. With the season quickly passing, and some weekends being completely free this would be very welcome business.

"Did you see the magazine spread of Seth at the beach, and those abs," Aunt Ida gasped, her eyes gleaming dreamily.

"His abs, really?" Vicky settled her gaze on her aunt and tried not to laugh. Aunt Ida's undying passion for handsome men was something that never failed to amuse her.

"Darling, just because a woman gets old she does not forget what a nice set of abs looks like," Ida winked heavily at her niece. "I can still spot 'em a mile away."

Vicky and Sarah shared a giggle as they watched their aunt prance away from the reception desk. Briefly they felt like the two sisters they had once been, carefree and best friends. But, things had changed when their parents died. They inherited the inn which they ran with Aunt Ida's help. They were still very close if not even closer than before even though they had very different lifestyles. Sarah was married with two sons while Vicky was still only dating.

"Do you think we can handle it?" Sarah asked as she glanced up at Vicky. "I mean, I don't want this to be too much pressure for us."

"I know we can handle it," Vicky replied with a smile.

"Okay, okay," Sarah nodded and then glanced at her watch. "Listen, I'm making dinner for Phil and the boys tonight. Why don't you and Aunt Ida join us?" Sarah asked hopefully. Sarah lived in a separate home off the inn property, while Vicky had an apartment in the inn and Aunt Ida lived in one of the guest rooms. Sometimes Sarah felt disconnected from them and wished they were all under one roof. But only sometimes.

"Sure," Vicky nodded with a slight smile. They hadn't had dinner together in ages and she was excited at the idea of seeing her brother-in-law and her nephews.

"Great," Sarah nodded and started to pick up the phone, before hanging it quickly back up. "Oh you know what!" Sarah suddenly said as if she had just had a wonderful idea. "Why don't you invite Mitchell as well?" she tried to hide her sneaky smile.

Vicky shifted uncomfortably from one foot to the other at the mention of Mitchell. He was a deputy for the local Sheriff's office, and they had been dating on and off. Officially, it was on at the moment. She considered him to be her boyfriend, but they hadn't taken it much further than awkwardly agreeing to the labels. She still felt a little uneasy about their relationship, and wondered how a dinner with the family would go over. She knew that Mitchell would be just fine, it was herself she was worried about.

"If I can get a hold of him," Vicky nodded vaguely without wholly committing. "You know how busy he can be," she added to soften her words.

"Sure, best deputy in town," Sarah's smile brightened even further. She was very impressed with his polite demeanor and the way he insisted on her sister being safe. She had begun teasing Vicky about the man who was so obviously smitten with her. It was hard not to find him endearing with the combination of his southern accent and those amazing blue eyes. Sarah was married to the love of her life and wished that Vicky could find happiness like hers.

"Better than Sheriff McDonnell," Vicky agreed dismissively and attempted to ignore her sister's knowing smile.

"Well, Sheriff McDonnell is getting older," Sarah shrugged mildly as she tried to give everyone the benefit of the doubt, including her younger sister who had the opposite personality to her. Vicky had a rather fiery nature that often led her into the middle of trouble. "But try and get Mitchell to come tonight, okay?" Sarah pleaded. "I know that Ethan and Rory would love to meet a real-life deputy sheriff," she dangled the nephew card without hesitation.

"All right," Vicky relented reluctantly with a bit of a scowl. "Anything for the boys!"

Sarah smiled triumphantly, and Vicky tapped the counter. "Let me know the details for this wedding so I can start organizing it," she requested in a professional tone. "If it is really going to be this weekend there is a ton of stuff to do!"

"Sure will, right after we have dinner," Sarah said with a quirk of her brow, she knew how to blackmail her sister into making sure she came to dinner.

Vicky laughed at her sister's words but she nodded. "I'll be there, sheesh," she giggled again and waved to her sister as she headed off in the direction of her apartment.

***

Vicky's apartment was on the main floor of the inn. It had a large living room, a spacious kitchen, a small office, and a good sized master bedroom. She liked living right in the middle of the action. Not only that, she had access to a pool, the beautiful gardens that surrounded the inn, and room service! Not to mention the spectacular views of the beautiful mountains.

As Vicky stepped inside she was already dialling Mitchell's number. They tended to play phone tag throughout the week and most of the time managed to get together on the weekends. He really did have a lot to handle as Sheriff McDonnell considered him his right hand man, while also watching him like a hawk. Mitchell had confided in her that he often felt as if the sheriff was just waiting for him to make a mistake so that he could pounce on him, and make him feel like a rookie officer again. Vicky was glad she didn't have to deal with that on a daily basis, and wondered how Mitchell tolerated it.

Mitchell had grown up in the deep south, and had moved to the area only a couple of years ago. They got along very well, but Vicky still held him at arm's length. She didn't want to be pressured into an official commitment. Mitchell on the other hand was not to be deterred. He was honest to a fault and had made no bones about telling Vicky that he wanted the opportunity to get to know her much better.

"Hello?" Mitchell's harried voice answered the phone on the second ring.

"Hi there, I thought I'd get your voicemail," she admitted with an awkward laugh.

"Oh, well, did you want me to take a message?" he suggested in a playful tone.

"Ha, ha," Vicky replied dryly and tried to hide a giggle. His jokes were often cheesy but she still liked them. There was something about his voice that made her feel cheerful. "I was wondering if you might be available this evening to come to dinner..." she started to say.

"Absolutely," he said abruptly, interrupting her.

"At my sister's," Vicky finished, and was greeted with silence on the other end of the phone. She waited a moment and then checked to make sure the call was still connected. "Mitchell, are you there?"

"Is this it then?" he asked when he finally began to speak again.

"Is this what?" Vicky asked with confusion. She wondered if she had upset him somehow.

"Is this the official introduction to the family?" he inquired rather gleefully. She could hear the anticipation in his voice, and realized he was reading a lot more into this than she had expected.

"Uh," Vicky hesitated, wondering if there was a way to soften the blow that she didn't consider the dinner to be a gateway into the next stage of their relationship.

"This is great," he said eagerly before she had the chance to correct him. "Of course I'll be there, what time?"

Vicky was silent as she tried to process what had just happened. She hadn't intended for it to be an official introduction, and what exactly did that mean?

"Six," she managed to say as her mind still spun around the implications of a family dinner.

"I'll be there," he said happily. "Can't wait to see you, Vicky," he added, before hanging up the phone.

Vicky stared at the phone for some time after he hung up. Had she just unintentionally sped up the development of their relationship?

Chapter Two

Oddly, as Vicky prepared herself for dinner that evening, she felt nervous. She wasn't sure what to wear. It was just dinner at her sister's, and yet it felt as if she was about to walk the runway for some reason. This was exactly why she tried to avoid serious relationships. Finally, she settled on some jeans and a button-down blouse. When she looked in the mirror she wasn't very satisfied, but she knew it would have to do for the night. The contents of her closet were spread all over her bed and bedroom and she would have to settle on something.

Vicky was still feeling a little anxious when she arrived at Sarah's house. When she opened the door and let herself in, Vicky found herself immediately assaulted by the surprisingly strong and unyielding grasp of her nephew, Ethan. He was only five, but the child seemed to know all there was about take downs. Vicky suspected Aunt Ida had been teaching him some Jujitsu behind Sarah's back. Aunt Ida had experience in a little bit of everything, from the martial arts, to pottery, to parachuting.

"Hey there," Vicky choked out and patted Ethan's blonde hair gently. "Good to see you champ," she said with a smile as he released her and she was able to breathe again. Just as she took a breath, her three year old nephew, Rory came ploughing towards her. She braced herself, and let out a quiet grunt when he slammed into her stomach.

"Ethan, don't hurt Aunt Vicky," Sarah called from the kitchen with laughter in her voice.

"It wasn't me, it was Rory!" Ethan shouted back with a pout.

"It's okay," Vicky called back. "I survived."

Rory grinned up at her devilishly. "Hello to you, too," she smiled at him.

As the boys ran off to finish their current favorite television show, Vicky was drawn to the lovely scents that were drifting from the kitchen.

"Oh Sarah, everything looks great," Vicky said as she stepped inside and offered her the loaf of French bread she had picked up at the store. "I hope this will go well."

"It's perfect," Sarah agreed and gave her a younger sister a quick hug before tending to the boiling pasta on the stove.

"You look nice this evening," she cooed. "I guess that means that Mitchell said yes? Hmm?" she winked at her sister.

"Yes, he said yes," Vicky sighed as she picked at a bit of cheese. "He's acting so strange though."

"Strange how?" Sarah asked and smacked her sister's hand away from the cheese. "That's for everyone," she said sternly.

"He seems to think that tonight is a big deal," Vicky explained hesitantly. "You know officially meeting the family."

"Isn't it?" Sarah asked as she tasted the sauce she was simmering. "Mm, here," she held out the wooden spoon for Vicky to try. Vicky had a taste and sighed with pleasure.

"Perfect, as usual," she mumbled.

"Thanks," Sarah laughed as she studied her sister. "Come on, out with it, what's really bothering you?"

"Well, why can't things just be good as they are?" Vicky asked with a frown. "Why do they always have to progress, and get messy?"

"They're supposed to progress because people have feelings, and those feelings grow stronger with time," Sarah explained patiently as if Vicky was asking a simple and obvious question. "It's so wonderful you don't even notice that it's messy."

Vicky shivered a little. "I guess it's just not my style," she frowned. "I just don't want Mitchell to get hurt because we have different ideas of what we want."

"Hmm," Sarah nodded a little. "Or maybe you're just afraid, that things are progressing whether you like it or not."

Vicky started to open her mouth to argue with her sister, when there was a knock on the front door.

"That must be Mitchell," Vicky said with relief. She was glad to avoid the unfolding conversation. Vicky stepped away from the kitchen to answer the door, but Sarah's words stayed in her mind. When Vicky opened the door an irresistible smile of excitement rose to her lips.

"Look who I found," Mitchell said, his fierce blue eyes shining as he smiled at her. Aunt Ida was snuggled up next to him, her arm tucked through his and a wide grin splayed across her full lips.

"I swear officer, I didn't do it," she lifted one set of long fingers to cover her mouth as she giggled. "Oh please, who's going to buy that?" she laughed out loud.

"Aunt Ida," Vicky said with a playful grin. "Come on in," she stepped back and held the door open for Mitchell and Ida to step through.

Aunt Ida reluctantly relinquished his arm so that Vicky could embrace him. When his lips sought hers, she pulled back slightly. He met her gaze questioningly, but that question was answered when Ethan popped his head up between the two of them.

"Are you Aunt Vicky's boooooyfriend?" he asked with a mischievous gleam in his eyes that were the same bright green as his aunt's.

"Uh well," Mitchell cleared his throat and then dropped down to the boy's eye level, a move that impressed Vicky.

"I don't know, what would you think if I was?" he asked curiously. Sarah had stepped into the living room to observe, and was whispering to Aunt Ida about how sweet Mitchell was.

"Hmm," Ethan narrowed his eyes as he scrutinized the man before him with all of the seriousness of a grown man. "You don't seem like the last guy on earth," he concluded.

"What?" Mitchell asked with confusion and glanced up at Vicky for help. Vicky's eyes widened some as she tried to anticipate what he was going to say next. She had to remember the kid liked to repeat things, this was something she could never seem to grasp.

"Well, Aunt Vicky said that she would only get married if there was only one man left on earth," Ethan declared happily. "So, I guess you're not her boyfriend," he shrugged and seemed to be satisfied by his own deduction.

"Oh, Ethan," Sarah gasped and grabbed her son gently by the arm to tug him away from Mitchell who had glanced up with curiosity at Vicky. Vicky could only stare down at him uncertain as to whether she should defend herself.

"Kids," Aunt Ida volunteered as she noticed her niece squirming. "They say the strangest things," she laughed lightly and Sarah soon joined in, hoping to break the mild tension that had formed.

"Yes, they do," Mitchell laughed as he stood back up and slid his arm around Vicky's waist.

"Sarah, these are for you," he added as he held out a small bouquet of flowers.

"Oh, thank you so much," Sarah gushed as she took the flowers and carried them into the kitchen to put them in water. When Mitchell glanced over at Vicky, he couldn't hide his smile of amusement

"Last man on earth, hmm?" he murmured beside her ear.

"Well," Vicky hesitated. Her opinion hadn't really changed that much. As lovely a marriage as Sarah and Phil had, she considered herself to have her Aunt Ida's spirit, free and wandering.

"I'm just kidding," he assured her and kissed her cheek softly. As they gathered around the kitchen table Sarah finished preparing their meal with the assistance of Ethan.

"Sorry guys it looks like Phil is running a little late," she sighed as she slid the ravioli onto a serving dish. "He's been busy lately, sometimes it's like we're passing ships rather than husband and wife," she laughed, but Vicky could sense the sadness in Sarah's voice. Phil had taken on some extra hours since the inn had not been producing as much income as it usually did. Aunt Ida was toying with her cell phone, she even turned it upside down once and shook it.

"What are you doing?" Vicky laughed as she watched her aunt getting more and more aggravated by the device.

"How do you get the texts out of these things?" she asked, obviously stumped by the tiny buttons on the phone. She was very intelligent, but she didn't handle technology too well.

"Here," Vicky took the phone from her and showed her the steps to access her text messages. "It's pretty simple," she said and then frowned as she hit the wrong button. "Well, I guess it could be simpler," she laughed a little and handed the phone back.

"Thanks sweetie," Aunt Ida said with a sigh of relief. She began scrolling through all of the messages that she had missed.

"Yes!" Aunt Ida shrieked with joy. "Yes! Yes! She can fit me in!"

"Who?" Sarah laughed as she added the French bread to the table and glanced towards the door once more.

"There's no time to waste," Aunt Ida announced as she stood up from the table. "I have an emergency appointment to get my hair done," she said and ran her fingertips through the short strands with a slight frown. "It's such a mess right now and luckily Sandra's new hairdresser has time to do it."

"You haven't even eaten," Vicky protested with a frown.

"Sweetheart, beauty waits for no one," Aunt Ida announced dramatically.

"Your hair looks wonderful," Sarah said with a sigh as she studied her aunt. "Everything about you always looks wonderful," she added as she tugged a stray feather out of her own hair. "I've been working on some costumes for Ethan and Rory, and I can't yet figure out how I have more feathers on me than on the parrot costumes," she laughed.

"I don't know how you ever have the time to do all of that," Vicky said as she plucked the feather from Sarah's hand. Just then the front door swung open and Phil called out from the living room.

"Never fear, Phil is here!" Phil walked up to the table to join them with a wide grin. "Sorry I'm late," he added as he leaned over to kiss Sarah gently on the lips.

"Ew," Ethan complained and covered his eyes. Rory just wiggled out of his chair and hid under the table.

"It's a team effort," Sarah said with a sweet smile at her husband. Vicky glanced over at Mitchell who seemed to be enjoying the banter between family members. Vicky loved her single life. She liked the idea of being free to wander as she pleased, but she still wondered sometimes if that would ever change. Sarah seemed to have everything, not only a normally successful business like Vicky but also an amazing husband and two beautiful children. The more Vicky got to know Mitchell, the more certain she was that if she were to ever have that life, she wanted it to be with him, but getting to that point at the moment seemed impossible. She just wasn't sure it was what she wanted. Was it fair to him to make him wait while she figured it out?

"Well, my hairstyle will hardly do for the guests we will have this weekend," Ida declared dramatically. "So, I really must be going."

She winked at Mitchell and leaned down to give him a peck on the cheek.

"When you see me again, I'll be twenty years younger," Aunt Ida said jokingly and kissed Phil on the cheek as well. Phil grinned at her with clear amusement as she spun on her heel.

"I don't see how you could get any more beautiful Aunt Ida, but if you insist," he said with the boyish charm that Sarah loved so much.

"Aw," Vicky giggled a little and Mitchell reached under the table to grab her hand, his gesture hidden by the tablecloth.

"Easy to see that such beauty runs in the family," he said mildly. His words were a bit of a surprise to Vicky as he could be a bit shy and wasn't usually one to attempt to be so charming. But, from the flushed cheeks of all three women, it seemed he had succeeded. "So tell me more about these special guests?" he asked hopefully.

"Yes, let's hear it," Phil said as he dropped down into a chair beside Sarah and reached across the table to ruffle Ethan's hair. Phil peeked under the table, "Rory, get out here," he said with a grin. Rory climbed back up into his chair but only sat in it for a second before he bolted over to his father for a big hug.

"Well, it's all very hush, hush," Sarah warned as she looked from Phil to Mitchell. Then she lowered her voice and grinned wildly. "But Seth and Trinie have decided to get married at the inn! Our inn!"

"Wow!" Phil said with surprise and sat back in his chair. "The actress Trinie?" he smiled with amazement. "We've seen plenty of wealthy people at the inn, but this is our first real super star. Just think of the publicity from that!"

"Not to mention Seth," Mitchell piped up and shook his head. "If only I could play tennis like that guy I might actually be able to beat the sheriff in one of our matches," he chuckled as he lowered his eyes with defeat. "That man has a mean swing."

"Oh well, Vicky is very good at tennis," Sarah said quickly as she added another piece of bread to Ethan's plate. He was not interested in the ravioli but he was enjoying the bread. "You should let her teach you sometime on the court at the inn," Sarah added as she met Vicky's eyes across the table. Vicky locked eyes with her sister and tried not to glare.

"I didn't know you could play tennis," Mitchell said with surprise as he looked at her.

"I'd like that, if you would teach me sometime," he looked at her eagerly.

"I'm not that great," Vicky said humbly and shot a scowl at her sister before she looked at Mitchell. "But if it means taking down the sheriff, I'm all for it."

Mitchell laughed and took a sip of his wine. "All right then," he agreed. "Maybe after the big wedding is over."

"Vicky is in charge of the whole thing," Sarah bragged openly. "From the cake, to the music, the dresses, everything!" Vicky felt a bit like she was being marketed, and though she knew her sister was doing it out of love it was beginning to annoy her.

"Do you think she can..." Phil started to ask, and Sarah swatted his shoulder to quiet him down. He cleared his throat as he realized his mistake. Vicky frowned as she looked down at her plate.

"She'll do fantastic," Mitchell said with confidence and gave her hand another squeeze under the table. "But if you need me for any reason, guests gone wild, or homicidal doves, feel free to call me, okay?" he met her eyes to make sure she understood he meant it.

"Yes," she nodded slightly, and grinned at the idea of doves attacking. "I'll keep you on speed dial," she assured him.

"I still can't believe it's really happening," Sarah admitted. "I remember watching Trinie when I was a kid on that Complete Teen show."

"Me too," Vicky grinned and the two sisters spoke at the same time. "Don't look in a magazine, get up to date with Complete Teen!"

Phil and Mitchell exchanged slightly horrified glances as the two women dissolved into giggles.

"I remember Trinie from when she was a little bit older," Phil said casually. "That movie, about the fountain."

"Oh really," Sarah cleared her throat and smiled at him. "What part do you remember?"

"Well uh, the fountain," he replied with a light smile.

"Mmhm, what was the movie about Phil?" she asked, teasing him.

"Something about a fountain, all I know is she ended up splashing in it!"

"Oh, that was her?" Mitchell said with surprise. "I didn't realize that!"

"You two are terrible," Vicky laughed. "Don't forget about Seth. I've never seen a man look so good in tennis whites," she winked at Sarah.

"Oh, but we haven't played tennis yet," Mitchell pointed out with a sly smile.

"Good point," Vicky laughed and finally began to relax as they shared their meal.

"So, what am I in for?" she asked Sarah. "Swans? Tigers? A parade?"

"No nothing like that," Sarah shook her head. "She did ask for pink roses, and she likes the idea of silver and white for the color scheme. Oh and musicians, she wants live music."

"Well, that's not too bad," Vicky said with surprise. "It sounds pretty simple."

"The place is going to be crawling with security," Sarah sighed. "It's almost impossible to keep something like this secret, so we're going to have to plan for lots of press showing up and trying to disrupt the ceremony."

"Well, if you'd like I can check with Sheriff McDonnell and see if we can spare a few officers to help with security," Mitchell suggested, gaining him a smile of relief from Sarah.

"That would be great. It would be wonderful if we had a few local officers to rely on."

"Absolutely," Mitchell nodded and finished off his wine. "I'll ask him first thing in the morning," he paused a moment before continuing. "Speaking of which, I should probably get going. I have the early shift tomorrow."

"I'll walk you out," Vicky offered and stood up from the table with him. "I better get going, too." She hugged Ethan and Rory and gave Phil and Sarah a kiss on the cheek goodbye. "Thanks for dinner."

"Thanks for joining us Mitchell," Phil called out and reached out to shake his hand. Mitchell gave it a quick shake and then nodded at Sarah.

"Thanks so much for dinner and the company ma'am, everything was delicious."

"Ma'am," Sarah giggled and waved her hand at him. "Any time, any friend of Vicky's is a friend of ours," she added with a small smile.

"True," Phil nodded.

"Are you sure you're not the last man on earth?" Ethan asked and reached for another slice of French bread.

"Ethan," Sarah hissed.

Vicky was laughing as she walked out onto the driveway with her arm locked in Mitchell's. As soon as they were outside he pulled her closer against him. Tentatively he touched his lips to hers, requesting a kiss, which she willingly offered. The caress was sweet and subtle. The time between their encounters seemed to make these expressions of their affection that much more passionate, and Vicky found herself wondering how serious he was about going home.

"Want to stop by my apartment?" she suggested hopefully. "I have a new action flick."

"No," he said, though the word seemed to strangle him as he spoke it. "I would love to, but I know that you have a lot to get ready for. This is important to you Vicky, and I want you to know that I support you."

Vicky smiled a little. He always said the sweetest things, but sometimes she wished he'd be willing to be a little less cautious and kind, and a little more wild and free. Maybe that was what was holding her back from him.

"All right then, good night," she said quietly. He brushed her dark brown hair back lightly from her cheek and leaned in to kiss her again. This time the kiss lingered, and his arms wound fully around her waist as he drew her against him.

"Good thing the wedding is this weekend," he sighed as he released her and waved as he strode over to his car.

Vicky smiled to herself as she watched the car back out of the driveway. Then his words sunk in. The wedding was this weekend. The most famous wedding ever to be held at the inn, and it was mostly on her shoulders! Her eyes widened and she hurried to her car, mentally adding a hundred things to the to-do-list in her mind.

***

Vicky stayed up most of the night putting together different packages to suggest to the bride and groom. She had an idea of the simplistic wedding they wanted, but there were a few special details, such as the flowers and the catering that were a little more involved. When the sun rose she woke feeling drowsy, but very excited. She felt as if everything was coming together just fine. She decided to meet Sarah for a cup of coffee in the restaurant attached to the inn. As she was walking across the lobby to meet her, she encountered a woman with her head hidden in the bulky hood of a man's coat.

"May I help you?" Vicky asked with surprise when she saw the woman. It was very early for a guest to be walking in.

"No one can help me my dear," the woman replied with such hopelessness in her voice that it still took Vicky a few moments to recognize who it was.

"Aunt Ida?" she asked hesitantly.

"Formerly known as," Ida nodded sadly.

"What do you mean?" Vicky asked with a laugh. "What are you doing with that ridiculous jacket?"

"Let me explain," Ida said with that same devastated tone. "Never in my life have I experienced such a terrible hairdo," she sighed and then shook her head. "All I asked for were a few blonde highlights, just to give me a splash of youth, and what a mistake that was."

"Why?" Vicky asked suspiciously and reached up in an attempt to pull the hood back from her head.

"No!" Ida gasped and clung to the hood, holding it down as if her life depended on it. "No, don't let anyone see," she insisted desperately. "If it were not for the fact that she promised me that the color would fade, I would have had her shave it all off!"

"It can't be that bad," Vicky laughed and reached again for the hood.

"No!" she gasped and Vicky saw real tears rise in her aunt's eyes. "It's, it's," she sniffled a little and finally released the hood. "Purple," she whispered as the hood fell away revealing the bright purple tresses beneath.

"Oh my," Vicky covered her mouth to try to suppress a laugh, but she couldn't hold back. Aunt Ida looked a bit like a troll with the shock of purple hair, and she just couldn't get that image out of her mind. "It's not that bad," Vicky squeaked out. "It's a lovely shade, really." Aunt Ida yanked the hood back up over her hair and glowered at Vicky.

"It's not that bad?" she hissed in return. "I look like a grape, seriously Vicky, don't lie to me! If you want to laugh, laugh," she huffed and blinked to hide the tears that were forming in her eyes.

Vicky did want to laugh, very badly, but she resisted for the sake of her aunt's feelings. She didn't want to make her feel worse than she already did.

"What's going on ladies?" Sarah asked as she stepped out of her office and joined them in the lobby. She looked perky enough, but Vicky could detect the worry lines at the corners of her eyes. She was already anticipating the worst with the upcoming wedding.

"Aunt Ida got a new 'do," Vicky declared, knowing that she needed a little cheering up. She reached up and tugged the hood back from Aunt Ida's head.

"Vicky!" she shrieked and tried to cover her hair with her long thin fingers. Sarah's eyes grew as large as saucers as she looked at the brightly colored hair.

"Aunt Ida, what were you thinking?" she groaned and shook her head. "Purple is not the new blonde, no matter what anyone tells you!" she paused a moment and then looked at the woman suspiciously. "You didn't get anything pierced, did you?"

"No," Aunt Ida groaned with embarrassment. "It wasn't supposed to be purple," she growled with annoyance. "All I wanted were a few little highlights and look at what it has turned into. Sandra's new assistant used the wrong liquid and if they dye over it, it will dry it out too much and it will break and probably fall out."

"Oh well," Sarah hesitated a moment and reached out to lightly touch her aunt's fried hair. "It's not so bad really," she attempted to sound positive. "At least you won't be easy to overlook," Sarah pointed out, hoping to brighten her aunt's mood.

Aunt Ida sighed heavily and then nodded. "I guess you're right about that. I'm going to go and shampoo it a million times and hope it washes out," she huffed as she headed for the elevator that would take her back up to her room.

"Poor Aunt Ida," Vicky said quietly as the sisters stood beside each other, waiting for the elevator doors to slide shut. As soon as they did, they both burst out laughing so loudly that they had to lean on one another for support.

Chapter Three

The next two days flew by as everything was prepared and carefully planned out. Sarah had a lot to handle on the business end, and Vicky was overwhelmed with trying to secure the wedding cake, the catering, and the photographers.

The day before the wedding was buzzing with activity. All the private security hired by the couple had arrived early in the morning, well before the bride and groom. The bridal couple had invited a few family members and friends to attend a small rehearsal dinner in the restaurant prior to the day of the wedding, so all their rooms were being prepared. All the staff members had gathered together in the large conference room for an early morning pep talk from Sarah. The most important message she impressed upon the staff was one of restraint.

"Once the guests arrive, please, let's conduct ourselves in a polite and professional manner," Sarah said sternly as Vicky listened in. "I know that we're all excited to have celebrities in our midst, but they are people, too. Remember this should be one of the most important days of their lives, and we need to treat them with as much respect and kindness as we treat all of our guests. Understand?" she asked as she looked from face to face. Her eyes lingered for an especially long time on Aunt Ida, who was wearing a scarf over her purple hair.

"They chose us because we have such a great reputation for providing a quiet place to celebrate such a wonderful event, so let's make sure we live up to that reputation. That means that only those authorized to do so may go to the third floor. Understand?" she looked at each of the faces again. "Don't ask me who's authorized either," Sarah said sternly. "If you are authorized then you already know who you are, and if you aren't, then you don't need to know who is. There's plenty to get ready in the kitchen, the restaurant, and out in the garden where the ceremony will take place. Any needs that the couple may have when they arrive will be tended to by those who have been given the job to do so."

She paused a moment and checked a text on her cell phone before she looked back up at the gathered staff. "This isn't just a matter of your job people, if the security that Trinie and Seth have brought in with them catches you sneaking around they will not hesitate to deal with the issue. I want this to go smoothly, and I promise there's a bonus in it for all of you if we can just get through this weekend without incident. Okay?"

The members of staff nodded while Aunt Ida stared miserably straight forward. She was still not over the disaster of her hair. As the staff members filed out of the conference room, Vicky walked up to Sarah with a proud smile.

"Great job sis," she said with genuine admiration. "You really sounded like you have everything under control."

"Oh, I am so stressed out," Sarah gasped as she pointed to the text on her cell phone. "It looks as if they are going to arrive an hour early and they need five more seats for the rehearsal dinner tonight."

"No problem," Vicky said with confidence. "I planned for the possibility of an early arrival. Their room is already prepared, there are strawberries and champagne on ice, and the rehearsal dinner allowed for ten extra guests just in case," she smiled proudly.

"Wow!" Sarah said with surprise as she looked at her sister. "You really do have everything under control."

"You shouldn't ever doubt me," Vicky replied, her smile spreading into a grin. "Little sisters do grow up too, you know."

Sarah smiled affectionately at her. "I know, but your big sister will always be here, don't forget that."

"I won't," Vicky assured her. Sarah grimaced as she saw another group of security guards walk past the glass doors of the conference room. It made Sarah uneasy as she watched them pile into the inn.

"Maybe this wasn't a good idea," Sarah frowned as she watched the handful of well-toned men walk past her.

Aunt Ida sighed with a smile as she watched them walk past. "I think it was a grand idea," she declared and followed after the men.

"Don't worry about it," Vicky said whilst giving her sister's shoulder a light squeeze. "The officers that Sheriff McDonnell is sending to help will be here soon, they can deal directly with the security guards, okay?"

Sarah nodded, and smiled at her sister. "I feel like you're the calm one in all of this Vicky, thanks."

"Hey for once I am," Vicky laughed. "Don't expect it to happen again." As she walked into the restaurant to check on the set up for the rehearsal dinner, her phone began to ring. She answered it after the first ring, knowing that it was likely wedding business.

"Hello? Vicky speaking," she said cheerfully. That cheerfulness quickly faded.

"What do you mean the photographer can't make it?" Vicky hissed into the phone. From across the room, despite the amount of harried staff that were running back and forth with vases, and tablecloths, Sarah seemed to sense that something was wrong. She locked eyes with Vicky, who quickly turned away. She didn't want Sarah to think anything was wrong, but losing the photographer who was handpicked by the bride and groom, was a pretty big problem.

"No, that isn't going to work," she said angrily into the phone when the receptionist offered to reschedule. "Don't you have anyone who you call when one photographer can't make it?" she demanded with her anxiety building. Sarah had begun to walk across the room towards Vicky when Vicky quickly nodded her head. "Okay fine. Email his details and I'll get approval from the couple. If there's a problem I'll let you know. But, as long as he has had the preliminary security check, that should be fine. I'll get back to you as soon as it's approved. Get him ready so that when I get back to you he can leave immediately," she growled into the phone and hung up just as Sarah reached her side.

"Something wrong?" Sarah asked as she studied her sister.

"No, no," Vicky shook her head quickly. "Everything is fine, right as rain, it's all good," she stopped herself as she realized how many words she had rattled off in such a short period of time.

"Vicky, tell me the truth," Sarah pleaded. "If this whole thing is going to fall apart, I'd rather know about it ahead of time."

"It won't," Vicky promised her and clutched her phone tightly. She hoped she wasn't lying to her sister. "It was just a snafu with the photographer, but as soon as we get the approval from Seth's assistant they're sending someone new out." Her phone beeped and she checked her emails. "That's the email from them already. I'll just forward it to Seth's assistant for approval," Vicky said while forwarding the email.

"Oh, okay," Sarah said with relief. "At least the groom didn't call off the wedding."

"I don't think Seth would ever do that," Aunt Ida said as she joined her nieces in the restaurant. "He's one of those good guys that you should never let get away, Like Phil or," she cast a knowing smile in Vicky's direction, "Mitchell."

"Aunt Ida, we're not that serious..." Vicky began to correct her, but Aunt Ida tilted her head towards the entrance of the restaurant.

"No, I mean, there's Mitchell," she said with a smile.

Mitchell was walking into the restaurant, his eyes wide at the transformation that had taken place over just a few days. A few officers followed after him as he walked across the restaurant towards Vicky.

"Hey," he smiled at her as he looked around at all she had created. "Great job, this place looks amazing."

"Thanks," Vicky replied and tilted her head towards the officers. "Thanks for the reinforcements too, things are really starting to get a little crazy."

"Of course," he nodded and caught her hand in his. "Just call me if you need anything," he held her eyes for a long moment.

"I will," she assured him and leaned forward to lightly kiss his cheek. As he walked off to make sure that the officers were introduced to Sarah, Vicky watched with admiration and that undeniable warmth that had been building in her chest. She checked her emails and Seth's assistant had already got back with approval. Very efficient, she thought as she sighed with relief. She quickly sent an email to the photographers to say that they could go ahead and send the new guy.

Vicky glanced at her watch and hoped that the photographer would not take too long to arrive. With all of the activity occurring inside she decided to look over the progress of the garden. It was being transformed into an elegant mixture of pale silvers and pure white hues, per the bride's request. It was a very appealing color combination as it drew and reflected the shimmering of the morning sun. She soon heard someone following behind her. A glance over her shoulder revealed it to be Aunt Ida. Her hair was still covered by a colorful scarf that accentuated the fine gown she wore.

"You're awfully dressed up," Vicky laughed a little as she watched her aunt approach.

"Well, they will be arriving today, won't they?" Aunt Ida asked with gleeful anticipation.

"Yes," Vicky nodded. "In fact they're coming earlier than expected. They should be here within the hour."

"Wonderful!" Aunt Ida said happily. "So please, give me something to do," she pleaded.

"You just want to stick around," Vicky grinned at her but pointed to the chairs that were being arranged. "Could you make sure they're spaced evenly apart?" she suggested. "I don't want the guests having to rub elbows."

"Absolutely," Ida headed for the chairs. As she was walking towards them a sudden gust of wind blew through the garden. It knocked into the tents that had been set up, ruffled the flowers that were being hung from the bushes and trees, and ripped the scarf right off the top of Aunt Ida's head!

"Oh no!" she cried out as various staff members hurried around her to make sure the tents stayed in place and the flowers didn't fall. None of them chased after her scarf. Her purple hair was exposed for everyone to see, and in particular, the photographer who had just arrived.

"Trend-setting granny," the photographer announced and snapped a photograph of Ida's purple hair.

"Granny?" Ida sneered as she turned on the man. "You have no right to call me that. I am in fact, nowhere near being a grandmother," she narrowed her eyes at him and began advancing upon him. The photographer slowly lowered his camera, realizing his grave mistake far too late.

"Ma'am, I didn't mean anything by it," he said quickly.

"Ma'am is it now?" Ida demanded as he was backed carefully into the wedding arch. "You must understand young man, that if I wanted to be in your little pictures, it would not be in this gown," she flicked the skirt of her gown dismissively.

"Aunt Ida, I'll get you another scarf," Vicky said quickly as she hurried over to the two. She didn't need another photographer bailing on her especially on the day before the wedding.

"Here, she can use this one," a soft, unassuming voice said from just behind her. Vicky turned to find Trinie standing there with Seth's arm laid casually across her shoulders. The pair was trying to look incognito but Vicky immediately recognized them. Trinie was holding out a lavender scarf that she had unwound from around her neck.

"It'll go nicely with the shade," she smiled as Aunt Ida stared at her absolutely star-struck.

"Thank you," Ida stammered as she accepted the scarf. "It's beautiful," she added. Vicky helped her tie it around her hair before she turned back to face the couple.

"It's a pleasure to meet you," Vicky said. "I'm Vicky, I know we've talked briefly on the phone."

"Oh yes," Seth nodded as he studied their surroundings from behind a pair of dark sunglasses. "I hope you don't mind our early arrival, it's just, we're both so excited," he admitted.

"Of course not," Vicky's smile spread into a grin. "Would you like me to show you to your room?"

"Perfect," Trinie nodded and winked at Aunt Ida who had yet to find her voice again. The photographer was snapping pictures of the encounter. Vicky watched him for a long moment. She hoped he would be as good as the original photographer. In the whirlwind of the rest of the afternoon, Vicky caught brief glimpses of the photographer snapping away as the guests for the rehearsal dinner arrived. Some were celebrities that she recognized, while others seemed to be just close friends or family members of the couple. All were escorted by security past the throngs of press that had begun to gather outside the gates of the inn. Someone had already tipped them off about the wedding, which was no surprise.

Vicky grew more nervous when the rehearsal dinner began. She had made sure that Henry, the head chef, had everything that he needed to create a successful and delicious meal. Sarah kept poking her head into the kitchen to check on things as well. Trinie and Seth were surrounded by people they loved, who they assumed loved them in return. It was a beautiful evening, with lots of heartfelt toasts, and hilarious memories shared.

The one time Vicky was sure that the night was a success was when Seth stood up and in front of the entire gathering proposed to Trinie again. There was a tense moment when Trinie hesitated to accept. But her playful grin indicated that she was just teasing him, and when she did accept, the entire group erupted into applause. Vicky was someone who tended to assume that most celebrities were stuck up or spoiled, but by the end of the night she was wishing for nothing but happiness for the sweet couple. If Trinie and Seth could take the risk knowing how long most celebrity marriages lasted, wasn't it something she should begin to consider?

***

After the rehearsal dinner was over, Vicky headed back to her apartment. She found Mitchell waiting for her outside the door.

"Hi," he said shyly as she smiled at him with surprise.

"What are you doing here?" she asked as she paused beside him.

"I'm sorry, I know that you're probably worn out, and it's the big day tomorrow. I was just hoping we could spend a few minutes together," he shrugged mildly. "If it's not a good time, I can go though," he offered

"No, it's fine," she smiled and opened the door. "Come on inside," she stepped in and waited for him to follow after her. They hadn't really done much hanging out at each others' places yet. Just the occasional after date drop off, but no evenings in. Mitchell nervously stepped inside and she closed the door behind him. Luckily, she tended to keep her place pretty neat, but she still glanced around wondering if something embarrassing might be in plain sight.

"Want a glass of wine?" she offered as she headed for the kitchen.

"If you're having one," he nodded slightly and sat down on the couch. As she poured them both a glass of wine she wondered why he might be there. Was it just to spend some time with her or was it because of what Ethan had said? It was hard not to think that the little boy's innocent words hadn't disturbed Mitchell at all. When she returned to the living room with glasses in hand he was sitting forward on the couch waiting for her.

"Thanks," he murmured as he accepted the glass of wine and she settled down on the couch beside him.

"So, what brings you here?" she asked as she reached out to lightly trace the slope of his shoulder.

"I just wanted to make sure that you were ready for tomorrow," he said calmly. "I thought you might like a massage."

"A massage?" Vicky grinned. "That sounds wonderful."

"Here," he shifted on the couch so he could reach her shoulders and gently rub them for her. His thumbs traced slow circles along her muscles, encouraging them to relax. "Everything is going to be perfect," he assured her. "Don't let yourself get worried."

"Right now I couldn't worry about anything," she purred as she unwound beneath his touch. There was something so loving about the way his fingertips sought out the tight areas of her shoulders and upper back.

"Good, remember that," he chuckled warmly, "because I want you to think about something."

Immediately Vicky began to tense up again. "What?" she asked hesitantly.

"I'd like to take you away for the weekend. Sometime soon," he suggested. "Maybe after this wedding is over, we could get a few days to ourselves, hmm?"

Vicky sighed as his fingers found just the right spot on her shoulders to relax her once more. "Do you really think you could stand me for two whole days?"

"Oh," he leaned forward slightly and whispered in her ear. "I think I could stand you for much longer than that," he assured her and then kissed her cheek softly. "Just think about it Vicky, you don't have to answer me now."

"Okay," she sighed as he drew his hands away from her shoulders and she sunk back against his chest. "If I say yes will I get another massage?" she asked hopefully as she looked up at him.

"As many as you like," he promised with a warm smile. "Now, I want to let you rest. But promise me, you're actually going to sleep, and not end up pacing all night going over your lists?"

Vicky sat up on the couch and studied him for a moment. It amazed her that he really did know her very well.

"I promise," she grinned and they stood up together. She walked him towards the door and found herself having to resist asking him to stay. When he leaned in for a lingering kiss, she nearly did, but he pulled away.

"Goodnight," he smiled at her. "I'll see you in the morning."

"Goodnight," she called out and watched him walk out of the side entrance of the inn. As she saw the door fall shut behind him, she had a strange thought. What would it be like not to have to say goodnight?

Chapter Four

Vicky's alarm went off early the next day. She wanted a good start so that she could check on things. She hurried to dress and headed out into the crisp morning air. The weather was supposed to be perfect, but that couldn't always be counted on. She double checked the tents to make sure that they were secure. Then she continued to evaluate everything that was needed for the day. So far she had discovered that the wine was not being chilled, and the cake had been delayed by an hour. She averted both crises quite easily.

Vicky decided to take a walk around the grounds and gardens to make sure that nothing was out of place from the set up the day before. As she rounded the corner of the inn she noticed that the flowers that lined the building were crumpled. They usually looked pristine. As she stepped closer, she spotted a shiny black shoe laying in the daisies. It was hard to see from a distance.

"Oh no," she gasped and wondered if one of the groomsman was drunk and had thrown his shoes out a window. What she saw next, partly hidden by the daisies was a sock wrapped around a foot. She began to tremble as she saw the wide open eyes of a man gazing endlessly up at the morning sky. The scream stuck in her throat as she realized this man was dead. It was the photographer who had come at the last minute as a replacement.

"Help," she squeaked out barely able to hear her own voice. "Help!" she cried out louder the second time as she reached for her cell phone. She called Mitchell as some of the inn staff came running towards her.

"Mitchell, I need you here, now," she gasped into the phone. As he listened to her words, he started heading out of his office.

"Let's go Sheriff, something has happened out at the inn," he called out as he hurried past the older man.

"I'm on my way, Vicky," Mitchell said firmly into the phone. "Just stay put, I'll be right there!"

Vicky was beside herself as she waited for Mitchell's arrival. Was this really happening? How was this possible? Was she dreaming? This was not the first dead body she had found in the gardens of the inn.

She did her best to steer all the guests away from the area. Sarah was the next to arrive, and when she heard about the discovery, she reacted just as Vicky had expected her to.

"That's it, we're going to have to call off the wedding," she announced dramatically and shook her head. "This will be the end of the inn." She wrung her hands and groaned. "I know, I know, that shouldn't be what I'm thinking of now, I should be thinking of that poor man who's lost his life, but I just can't!"

"Sarah, take a breath," Vicky said firmly as she settled her gaze on her sister. "This is something none of us could have predicted. It's happened. It's terrible. But it doesn't mean we have to cancel the wedding," she insisted.

"Vicky, how can you even say that?" Sarah demanded as she stepped closer to her sister. "Someone is dead, and the ceremony is in just a few hours. How long do you think it's going to take the police to process the scene? Do you really think Trinie is going to want pictures with red and white flashing lights in the background?"

"Please, just wait before you cancel the wedding," Vicky said with despair in her voice. If Seth and Trinie didn't want to cancel the wedding, and the police didn't make them cancel the wedding she knew that her sister would be the one to decide in the end, but she couldn't imagine disappointing Trinie and Seth. "The body is nowhere near the wedding garden, the police can still conduct their investigation. The ceremony isn't until nearly sunset, so we have time to clear this up as much as possible." Vicky knew that it would be hard to convince her sister, but she was determined to try.

"I don't know, Vicky," Sarah hesitated as she glanced in the direction of the garden where the ceremony would be held. It was a good distance away.

"If we cancel the wedding, the reputation of the inn will be jeopardized," Vicky reminded her older sister with urgency in her tone. "If we go through with the service, and everything goes as planned, then we've lost nothing. Trinie and Seth will have their happy day, the guests won't be disturbed, and the crime, if it is a crime, will still get solved."

Sarah sighed and nodded slowly. "You're right," she reluctantly agreed. "But if anyone is in danger or the police say that we have to cancel it we're going to need to come up with a plan."

"Okay but just think of all the security that's here," Vicky pointed out with confidence. "This has to be the safest place around."

"Ahem," Sheriff McDonnell cleared his throat behind her. "Tell that to the man who is dead in the daisies."

Vicky turned to face him and drew a deep breath. Sheriff McDonnell's shirt was stretched to the point that the buttons were strained enough to reveal the white undershirt beneath. He wore his pants high up on his waist, and stood with his shoulders held back to show off the Sheriff's star pinned to his chest. His entire life had been defined by working in law enforcement. "Do you know how he ended up there?" he inquired brusquely.

"I've got no idea what happened," Vicky said quickly. "I found him just a little while ago when I called Mitchell. All I know is that he's a photographer, and he replaced the one who was meant to be here." She hesitated a moment and then pulled her phone out of her pocket. "I'll get you his name," she said as she searched for the email from the photography company.

Mitchell walked up to join them, and nodded his head respectfully at Sarah who was watching as several officers and medical personnel swarmed the area beneath the window. The sheriff looked up at the window above the flowers and rubbed his chin slowly.

"His name is Graham Walker," Vicky said. "I have details of the photography company but no more information on him."

"I'm sure he has ID in his wallet," Mitchell stated. He glanced up at the window as well. It was open wide with the curtains billowing through.

"Well, it's pretty obvious that he fell through the window," Sheriff McDonnell said quietly. "Poor fool was probably drunk, or maybe he was trying to get a closer look at the flowers," he muttered and arched an eyebrow. "Unfortunate event," the sheriff nodded as he walked towards the body.

Mitchell hung back and looked into Vicky's eyes. "Are you okay?" he asked her tenderly.

"I will be," Vicky nodded and managed a slight smile. The discovery of the body was weighing heavily on her mind, not just because of the wedding, but because this wasn't the first dead body she had discovered in the garden.

"It's going to be fine," he promised her. "I'm sure it was just an accident."

Vicky nodded, but she was not convinced.

"What do you make of this?" Sheriff McDonnell asked Mitchell as he stepped up beside him.

"Well, it could be an accident," Mitchell said quietly as he crouched down in front of the body. "Or even a suicide."

"Strange place to commit suicide," the sheriff muttered as he studied the man's wide open eyes. "Why come to an event like this if you planned to off yourself?"

"Media attention?" Mitchell suggested as he glanced back towards the gates that blocked the entrance of the inn. "Maybe he thought he'd get his name in the news, because of Trinie and Seth's wedding. Or maybe it's something simpler, a love affair?"

"You mean with the actress?" the sheriff asked with surprise.

"Well, actresses aren't exactly known for their fidelity, are they?" Mitchell asked with a light shrug.

"Maybe," the sheriff nodded and then glanced up at the window above the body. "It's certainly big enough for a fall, either intentional or unintentional. I imagine that the tox screen will reveal more."

"Boss, I don't see any bruising," one of the officers stated after looking over the body as thoroughly as he could.

"No defensive wounds," the sheriff nodded.

"Those can sometimes show up later," Mitchell pointed out in a professional tone.

"Sure they can," the sheriff nodded and then adjusted his hat. "But, I don't think that will be the case. Seems like it's pretty cut and dry." The sheriff waved his hand towards the officers under his command. "Conduct minimal interviews with the staff, do your best to avoid the guests," he glanced over to where Sarah and Vicky were talking quietly to one another. "This wedding has been a huge deal for the entire town, if we can keep this quiet, we will."

"His watch is smashed and the time on it is 10:25 pm," Mitchell told the sheriff as he bent over the body.

"It is possibly the time of death. The time he hit the ground," Sheriff McDonnell acknowledged.

"Sheriff, should I process the scene upstairs?" Mitchell suggested as he stood up.

"Yes. There are some officers already up there securing it," the sheriff nodded.

Mitchell nodded and headed into the inn. He didn't notice that Vicky was following quickly behind him, until she ducked into the elevator with him.

"Vicky," he frowned and met her gaze sternly. "You can't go into the room with me, you know that. This is an official investigation."

"I am aware of that," Vicky nodded innocently. "I just wasn't sure if you knew what room he was in…"

"Vicky," Mitchell firmly pressed the button to re-open the doors on the elevator. "I promise, I will keep you up-to-date. We are trying to process everything quickly so that the wedding can go ahead," he assured her.

"Fine," Vicky sighed and reluctantly stepped out of the elevator. As she rejoined Sarah outside to observe the forensic team, she was wondering if they found anything important in the photographer's room. She stared up at the window, watching for Mitchell's shadow to cross it. When he returned from the building she held her breath as he walked over to the sheriff and spoke to him in a low tone.

"I think this was a suicide or an accident," Sheriff McDonnell said loudly enough for them both to hear. "There's no reason to stir up more dust than necessary."

"I just want the chance to rule out all other possibilities," Mitchell replied, standing his ground while attempting to remain respectful.

"What's that about?" Sarah said in a hushed voice as she moved with Vicky.

"I don't know," Vicky frowned. "They don't exactly get along."

"I'm going to go and talk to Seth and Trinie to make sure they know what is going on and see what they want to do."

"What's going to happen with the wedding?" Vicky asked as she looked towards her sister.

"The sheriff said that this area and the room upstairs will be sealed off, but at the moment the wedding is still on as long as Seth and Trinie still want it to be on," she said as she hurried off.

The sheriff and Mitchell were still speaking, but more quietly. As Mitchell walked off in the direction of the inn again, Vicky fell into step beside him.

"Everything okay?" she asked as she glanced over at him.

"I think the sheriff is a little star-struck," he admitted with a shake of his head.

"Oh right," Vicky nodded with a smile.

"I am just going back to the room," Mitchell nodded.

"Well, I'll ride up with you, I want to check and make sure everything else is ok up there and then check in with Seth and Trinie," she smiled.

"Sure," he returned the smile.

They crossed the lobby and took the elevator to the third floor. As soon as they were alone in the elevator, Mitchell reached out to take her hand in his.

"Can't all go smoothly huh?" he glanced over at her.

"If it did, it wouldn't be my life," Vicky said with a sigh. He stroked the back of her hand and then gently squeezed it. "We'll get through this, don't worry."

"I'm trying not to," she frowned and then tilted her head slightly towards him. "I feel better now that you're here."

He smiled at that. "Careful now, or you'll have me thinking you really want me around," he warned her.

When they reached the third floor hallway one of the officers was waiting for Mitchell. "I was just coming to get you Deputy, we found something," he said as he joined Mitchell at the doorway to the photographer's room and as he swung the door open Vicky couldn't help but take a peak.

The room was neat, the bed still made as if it had not been slept in. The photographer's phone was sitting on the small table beside the bed. All of his expensive digital camera equipment was resting on the floor untouched. If anyone else was involved it certainly wasn't for the purpose of stealing valuables.

The officer walked with Mitchell over to the computer screen. Mitchell's eyes went wide as he looked at the screen. Vicky ducked down the hallway despite her desire to be more nosey. What was on that computer? As she walked towards Seth and Trinie's room she caught sight of the scene below through one of the windows in the hallway. She saw Sarah had already returned to the scene and was talking with a few members of the staff.

When she reached Seth and Trinie's room, she knocked lightly on the door. The door swung open beneath the knock, and she heard voices inside the room.

"I still don't think it could have been him," Seth was saying in an aggravated tone. "I mean, I trusted him, didn't you?"

"Sure I did," Trinie replied with a heavy sigh. "But with lives like ours Seth, you know we can't trust anyone. Someone probably waved a high enough pay check in front of him and he decided that protecting us wasn't worth missing out on millions," her voice rose with anger as she continued. "Every single time something good is about to happen in my life, something like this happens!" she growled. "How can we go through with the wedding after this?"

"You're not really thinking of calling off the wedding are you, Trinie?" Seth replied with shock. "We can't let one selfish creep stop us!"

As Vicky listened in on the argument she felt her heart sink. It sounded like they were talking about the photographer and from everything they were saying it was clear the wedding plans were in danger. She knocked again, this time a little harder. Both voices suddenly cut short. After a moment, Seth opened the door.

"Hi Vicky," he said glumly as he opened the door for her.

"Everything okay?" she asked him.

"No, everything is not okay!" Trinie announced as she marched out of the bedroom. "The wedding is off!"

"Is that because murder doesn't go well with wedding vows?" the sheriff's voice asked from the doorway.

"What?" Trinie stammered out as she looked from Seth to the sheriff. "What are you talking about?"

"Vicky you need to leave. I need to talk to Seth and Trinie in private," Sheriff McDonnell said in a stern voice.

Vicky left but she didn't close the door all the way and stood in the hallway trying to listen in.

"Look folks, I hate to do this," the sheriff said calmly as he studied them both. "Honestly I'm a fan," he nodded his head towards Trinie. "I didn't want anything to disrupt your special day. But, I can't overlook cold blooded murder."

"Murder?" Seth repeated looking just as dumfounded as his fiancée. "Why do you keep saying that?"

"We have reason to believe that the photographer, Graham Walker, was murdered," the sheriff informed them both coolly. "But one or both of you already knew that, didn't you?" he asked in a stern tone.

"Excuse me," Seth snapped as he stepped in front of Trinie. "You've no right to accuse us of anything. We were in our room all night, since after the dinner until now. There was a bodyguard in the hallway throughout the night. Besides that, why would we have anything against this photographer? We approved him."

Vicky narrowed her eyes as she recalled the argument the two had been having when she arrived at their room. She presumed it was about the photographer and wondered if Seth was truly going to lie to the sheriff about it.

"He has defensive wounds that are beginning to show and we found evidence on his computer that clearly indicates he had leverage over both of you. Photographs of you, Trinie, in a very compromising position. I believe you probably know what I'm talking about," Vicky's mouth dropped open in shock. "That's something we'll need to discuss further down at the station," Sheriff McDonnell said sternly.

"You're not really going to force us out of here in handcuffs in front of all of those reporters, are you?" Seth asked incredulously. "This is outrageous. Is this how law enforcement works in this town? We have an alibi for God's sakes! Matt, our bodyguard can confirm we were in our room."

"Just relax we are not arresting you, yet," the sheriff countered. "But, we have spoken to Matt and he cannot confirm that you were definitely in your room the whole night. He said that you told him he could take a break and he wasn't outside your room the whole time. You could have easily left your room and gone into the photographer's room without him seeing. So, if the only person who can confirm your alibi is your fiancée, and vice versa, then you do not have an alibi."

"There was also a woman, who brought us the champagne last night! She knows we were here, she spoke to us, even shared a glass with us," Trinie insisted.

'What woman?" the sheriff asked.

"The one with the purple hair," Trinie nodded with confidence. "I think she might work here."

"What time was she here?" the sheriff asked.

"From about ten until eleven o'clock," Seth nodded with a frown. "She was quite entertaining, but we wanted to get to bed early so we'd be ready for the ceremony today."

"Well, of course we'll have to verify the alibi and the time of death," the sheriff said with a sigh. "For now, just stay in your room, and do not contact anyone, okay?" he looked directly at both of them. "Whoever did this may have had something against you, and you need to exercise extreme caution."

"We'll make sure our bodyguards are on alert," Seth agreed, still offering the sheriff a blistering glare. He did not enjoy being accused of murder. The sheriff ignored the glare.

The sheriff stepped out as Vicky was walking down the corridor. "Vicky," the sheriff called. Vicky turned around with a smile, relieved she had not been caught right outside the door. "Please find your aunt and tell her I need to speak to her," he met her gaze with a quirked brow and she knew that she better not ask any questions and should find Aunt Ida fast.

"Sure," she nodded quickly.

Chapter Five

Aunt Ida was not usually hard to find. Vicky assumed that she would only have to follow the trail of handsome security guards to find her. To her surprise her aunt was nowhere to be found. As she made her way back through the lobby of the inn she spotted Ida and Sarah standing near the reception desk with Sheriff McDonnell.

"But all of the staff were told to stay off that floor," Sarah was saying as Vicky walked up to the trio.

"I made that clear to everyone," Sarah emphasized, her own expression darkened by the knowledge that someone had defied her direct instructions not to disturb the couple. Ida shifted from foot to foot, and then smiled at Mitchell as he joined them in the lobby.

"Would you like some tea, sweetheart?" she asked, laying on her thickest charm. "I'll just run and get us some," she said quickly and started to walk away.

Mitchell shifted his gaze towards her at the same moment that the sheriff, Sarah and Vicky did. Ida looked as if she was caught in the beam of headlights as her eyes widened innocently. "What?"

"Aunt Ida," Sarah growled and scrutinized the woman. "Did you take the champagne to them?" Vicky braced herself as she already knew that is what her aunt must have done.

Ida huffed and fluttered her hands at her sides as if she was searching for an excuse on her person. "Well, you said not to," she pointed out.

"And?" Sarah asked with a stunned chuckle. "That doesn't answer the question."

Mitchell stepped between the glowering sisters and their aunt. "Ida," he paused a moment and then offered her a slow, sweet smile. "May I call you, Ida?"

Ida's lashes fluttered lightly. "If you'd like," she agreed.

Vicky and Sarah exchanged knowing glances as Mitchell moved closer to Ida. "Listen, if it were me, I would have found a way to that room. I mean who wouldn't? The chance of a lifetime is sleeping under your roof, you have to get a little peak, right?"

Ida frowned uncomfortably but she reluctantly nodded. "Well, I couldn't help it, I just couldn't resist."

Sarah gasped from behind Mitchell and stepped around him with a finger jutting towards her aunt. "You did go up there!" Sarah exclaimed and pressed the heel of her palm to her forehead.

"Don't worry," Mitchell assured both of them. "This could actually be a very good thing," he turned back to Ida. "Now, when you went upstairs, did you notice anything unusual?"

Ida shifted uncomfortably again as the sheriff crossed his arms, and Vicky settled her eyes to her aunt's.

"Well, there was something unusual," Aunt Ida reluctantly confessed. "I went up the back stairs and when I was walking towards their room I saw Seth in the hallway with one of their bodyguards. Seth looked pretty angry. He kept saying, 'How could you do this to us?' So I hung back a little bit and waited."

"Then what happened?" Mitchell prompted her with interest.

"Well, the bodyguard was upset, he kept insisting that he had nothing to do with it, that it wasn't his fault. Then he said, he would make it right, to just give him another chance," Aunt Ida shook her head. "I mean I didn't want to seem too nosey"

"Did you see where the bodyguard went?" Mitchell asked hopefully.

"No, not really, he just stormed down the hall. I didn't really notice much, as Seth was in his undershirt and..." she sighed dreamily. Vicky considered Ida's words and the fact that Seth hadn't revealed the encounter with his bodyguard. So, that's why the bodyguard left his post and couldn't give them an alibi Vicky concluded. Was it possible they were arguing about the pictures that had been found on Graham's computer?

"Aunt Ida!" Sarah muttered disapprovingly and blushed with embarrassment.

"You would be distracted, too," Aunt Ida insisted.

"Anyway, I waited for a bit after Seth went back into the room. I planned to just hand them the champagne, but the poor guy looked so worried that I decided to stay and try to cheer them up. I'd hate to see such a lovely young couple throw away their chance at happiness over some squabble," she shook her head sadly.

"Wait, are you saying that Trinie and Seth were fighting?" Mitchell asked and stepped closer to Aunt Ida to ensure that he was hearing her correctly.

"Not exactly fighting," Aunt Ida corrected him with a slight frown. "It was more like a heated discussion. Seth was insisting that the bodyguard, Matt, I think he called him, had nothing to do with it, and Trinie was determined that he was mistaken. Anyway, it all ended when I showed up with the champagne, so I took it upon myself to attempt to lighten the mood," she fluttered her hands lightly in the air.

"And how long were you there?" Sheriff McDonnell asked with keen interest. "Just a few minutes?"

"No, no, had to be at least an hour," Aunt Ida sighed and then looked guiltily at Sarah. "But they wanted me to stay, Sarah. I wasn't bothering them, I swear," she looked at her niece pleadingly.

Sarah sighed and reached out to give her aunt a small hug. She knew that Aunt Ida was well meaning and loved the adventure.

"Well, as long as the time of death matches the time you're claiming to have been with Trinie and Seth then you've just provided them with an alibi," the sheriff stated. "I'm going to check on what forensic results have come through at the station, Mitchell, I want you to stay on top of this, understand?" he met the deputy's eyes with an authoritative glare.

"Yes sir," Mitchell nodded.

"I happen to enjoy that young lady's acting, and I want to make sure neither of them comes to any harm. If they had something to do with this, then justice will be served, until then consider them both to be under protective custody," he nodded his head to Sarah, Vicky, and Aunt Ida before turning to the front door of the inn. As he walked away Sarah wiped her hand across her face and grimaced.

"I knew this was going to be a bad idea," she groaned and shook her head.

"It's going to be fine," Vicky promised her, but she didn't even really believe that herself anymore. So far they had one dead body and evidence that pointed them in the direction of a celebrity couple that was meant to be married at the inn today.

"I'm going to take another look upstairs," Mitchell said and started to walk away. Vicky grabbed his arm gently to stop him. When he glanced back at her, she asked almost in a whisper.

"Is it true? Were there really pictures?"

"Yes," he nodded with a grave expression. "And not pictures she would have ever wanted getting out. I'm afraid, that until we can confirm beyond a doubt that the time of death occurred between ten and eleven o'clock, Trinie and Seth are still our best suspects."

Vicky nodded with dismay and released his arm as he headed for the elevator. She left Aunt Ida to go and get Sarah some calming herbal tea and decided to check that everything was ready for the wedding, if there was a wedding. As she walked into the kitchen she found the chef, Henry, staring out the window at the commotion.

"Henry?" she asked as she stepped up behind him. He nearly jumped out of his skin as he turned around to face her.

"Oh Vicky, I'm sorry, you startled me," he cleared his throat.

"Sorry to sneak up on you. Are you ok?" she frowned as she studied the concern on his face.

"Vicky, I feel so terrible," he gulped out and shook his head.

"What is it? What's wrong?" Vicky asked him and reached out to lightly touch his shoulder.

"Last night I heard a scream, I was getting ready to watch a show on TV, and I had just settled down with a bedtime snack. I heard this scream, and then a thump," he shook his head again. "I would have thought it was strange, I really would have, if it wasn't for all the media camped out. I figured one of them had just tried to make it over the gates. When I didn't hear anything else, I assumed it was fine, and I just went on watching my show," he shook his head again and moaned into the back of his hand. "To think I was snacking while someone lay dead in the daisies, but I didn't know!"

"It's okay, Henry," Vicky assured him as she patted his arm. "There was nothing that you could have done. Now the best thing you can do is tell the police about this, and what time it was when it happened."

"Oh yes, it was just before ten-thirty," he said with a quick nod. "I know it was, because that's what time the show comes on."

Just then Mitchell walked into the kitchen.

"Excuse me," he said in a professional manner. "I don't mean to interrupt, but I need to speak with Henry."

"Yes, good, I was going to come to speak to you," Henry said anxiously as he stepped forward.

"Really?" Mitchell asked with interest in his eyes. "What did you want to speak to me about?"

Vicky ducked out of the kitchen. Now that Seth and Trinie had been ruled out, who could it be? She wanted to check on Seth and Trinie and make sure that they were prepared for the wedding. Maybe she could also get another look at the photographer's room. As she stepped into the elevator and hit the button to close the doors, she was surprised when a hand stopped them from closing.

"Vicky," Mitchell said as he stepped into the elevator, "where are you headed now?" he asked, as if he didn't already know by the glowing circle around the number three.

"I was going to check on Seth and Trinie," Vicky said. "Make sure they are ready for the wedding."

"Vicky, make sure you and your Aunt Ida stay out of the case," Mitchell said as he turned to face her, pinning her between the back of the elevator and his lovely uniformed chest. "Anything you do here could contaminate the crime scene, the evidence and the witness testimony. If that happens, then we might never be able to prosecute the right person. This isn't just a normal case, it involves Trinie and Seth, and we have to make sure every base is covered."

"Of course," she sighed. Mitchell knew that Aunt Ida had a keen interest in reading murder mysteries that often translated into her coaxing Vicky into investigating real-life mysteries with her. However, at the moment Aunt Ida seemed to be too star-struck to worry about the murder.

When they reached the third floor and stepped off the elevator, Vicky noticed that the door to the photographer's room had been left open. There was police tape stretched across the doorway, but it had obviously been disturbed.

"Someone's been in there," Vicky said with a frown.

"I wonder what they were looking for?" Mitchell inquired as he peered into the room.

"Maybe the pictures?" Vicky suggested cautiously.

"The pictures have already been turned in, along with the computer and all of his camera equipment. Whatever it was, this person was looking for, I doubt they found it," Mitchell sighed as he walked towards the window that overlooked the gardens. The body had already been removed, but the memory of it being there was still imprinted on the minds of all those who had seen it. Vicky remained by the door.

"The truth is if Seth or Trinie wanted Graham dead, all they had to do was hire someone," Mitchell shrugged as he tucked his hands into his pockets. "It's not pleasant to think of, but it's the truth. With their wealth and influence they could easily get away with a hit."

"But why go to all the trouble of bringing him to the wedding?" Vicky asked, not convinced. Her mind kept travelling back to the argument she had overheard Seth and Trinie having as she knocked on their door. They were both acting as if they knew about the pictures, which should have made it obvious that they were the ones out to cause Graham harm. But she didn't believe they would do such a thing.

"They're hiding something," she finally said as Mitchell looked away from the window and back towards her.

"That's for sure," he agreed.

"But the question is, what?" Vicky pointed out.

"You mean other than murder?" Mitchell frowned. "Isn't that enough?"

"It's not murder," Vicky said with confidence. "I don't think they had anything to do with Graham's death."

"Vicky there are countless security guards here that for a little extra cash would have been willing to make Seth and Trinie's problem go away," he explained. "As of now even the inn staff are suspects. Money can make people do things that they never would have considered otherwise."

"Maybe," Vicky bit into her bottom lip and peeked down the hallway. "But celebrities aren't always the only ones that have everything to lose."

"What do you mean by that?" he asked with surprise. "Do you think someone else had a motive to go after Graham? The pictures were of Trinie, who else would care about them?"

"I don't know," Vicky admitted with a sigh.

Just as she spoke she was interrupted by voices from the end of the hall. Vicky looked down the hallway to see who was approaching. It was Seth and Trinie with a tall muscular bodyguard at their side.

"Hello," Vicky said as she stepped out further into the hallway with Mitchell right behind her. "I hope you guys aren't getting too stressed out."

"How could we with the complimentary massages your sister just treated us to?" Trinie said with a smile.

"Good, I'm glad you were able to relax a little," Vicky said quickly.

"I'll come and check on you guys in a minute. Make sure you have everything you need," Vicky said as they walked to their room. She wondered if this was Matt, the bodyguard that Seth had an argument with.

"Thanks, Vicky," Trinie nodded.

"I better call the sheriff," Mitchell sighed.

"I'll go see Seth and Trinie," she said as she turned and hurried down the hall.

Vicky nearly walked right into a maid who was headed into one of the adjacent rooms.

"Oh, so sorry Vicky," the maid, Emily, said.

"No, I'm sorry," Vicky smiled kindly at the woman. "I wasn't paying attention to where I was going."

"I'm just trying to tidy this room up very quickly, before he comes back," Emily said quickly as she stepped into the room. Vicky followed after her curiously.

"Whose room is this?"

"The bodyguards'," Emily said in a whisper, "Matt and the other bodyguard share it."

"Oh, you know them," Vicky questioned.

"Only Matt Castille. I can't actually believe that he is here," Emily said with a secretive smile as she straightened the sheets on the bed.

"What do you mean? Who is he?" Vicky asked with surprise

"Oh, I thought you knew. You see he's the same bodyguard who was involved with that young country singer, Charlotte. Have you ever heard her sing?" she sighed with pleasure as she recollected the melody. "She could sing so beautifully. But when that greedy bodyguard sold out to that photographer, and those pictures got out," she clucked her tongue lightly, "her career was over before it even really got started."

"Pictures?" Vicky asked curiously.

"Yes, pictures," the maid nodded. "Pictures of her doing things she shouldn't have been, with someone else's husband."

"Well, that's interesting," Vicky said with a grimace. She was beginning to see that there might be a pattern involved here. "Thanks for the information, Emily."

"Sure," Emily nodded and then flashed a smile at Vicky. "This has to be the most exciting wedding of the whole year. I still can't believe that we're all part of it."

"Me neither," Vicky agreed and gritted her teeth as she stepped out of the room. She could only hope that there would actually be a wedding. She headed the rest of the way down the hallway to Seth and Trinie's room. When she knocked on the door the bodyguard opened it.

"Let her in," Seth called out to him with a nod when he saw it was Vicky.

"Hi," she said as she walked into the living area of the suite. "Are you two doing okay? Do you have everything you need?"

"Sure," Trinie nodded and cast a worried glance in Seth's direction. "Just a little nervous."

The door to the room swung open and in walked another bodyguard. He had cropped brown hair, broad features, and wide shoulders. His biceps were bulging and muscular, and his black shirt was pulled taut across his chest and stomach. Vicky met his eyes as he paused just inside the door of the room.

"Oh good, that's Matt," Seth said with relief.

"Matt?" Vicky asked as she continued to stare at the man. Vicky realised that this was the bodyguard who Aunt Ida described as having the fight with Seth the night of the murder and the one who Emily knew about.

"His father used to work for me and he's been with us for some time now, and if it wasn't for him, we wouldn't be able to live the private life we do," he sighed with appreciation. Well, it looked like whatever the argument had been over between Seth and Matt had been resolved.

"He's really been amazing," Trinie agreed with a slight smile. "It's strange to have someone around specifically to guard your well being, but when you're in a position like we are, you need it. There's so many people out there seeking to hurt you," she added, a touch of sorrow settling into her voice. "To think, we thought..." she began to say.

"But we were wrong," Seth said quickly and met Trinie's eyes sternly. "So there's no need to discuss it."

"Oh right, of course," Trinie nodded a little. Vicky could tell there was something more unspoken between the two of them. Was it about the pictures?

"Are you two sure you want to go on with the ceremony?" Vicky asked with concern. "I don't want to put your safety at risk. We still have no idea who might have killed Graham."

"As long as Matt is with us, we'll be perfectly safe," Seth said with confidence. "Right Trinie?" he asked as he reached for her hand.

"Absolutely," she nodded and smiled at Vicky. "After all the hard work you've put into this, we're not going to let anything spoil our beautiful day."

Vicky was touched by their kindness and warmth, but she was also concerned. So far they had no idea who the killer was, or even exactly what the killer's motive might have been.

Mitchell was still entertaining the idea that it was a murder for hire, but there was no way Vicky could believe that Seth and Trinie were involved.

Chapter Six

Vicky returned to the lobby to find Sarah fielding frequent phone calls from the press.

"No, the wedding is not off, no further comment," she snapped and hung up the phone. "These reporters just won't stop!" she gasped out with frustration. "I couldn't even imagine what it would be like to have to deal with them all the time."

"Me neither," Vicky agreed as she paused beside the desk. She saw Mitchell walking towards her from the other side of the lobby.

"This whole thing is turning into a disaster," Sarah said testily as she tapped a few keys on the computer and tried to put out yet another fire with the kitchen staff over what exactly the menu was supposed to be. "We should have cancelled this morning, now it's going to be impossible."

Vicky frowned. "Seth and Trinie don't want to cancel," she pointed out. "I think we can still pull this off."

"I'm not sure," Sarah shot back. "I am concerned about the inn, the staff, and putting Seth and Trinie in more danger than they need to be."

"Now Sarah," Mitchell said speaking up before Vicky could argue. "I really don't think it's such a bad idea for the wedding to go on. Vicky made a good point. Here Seth and Trinie are surrounded by security, police, and even reporters recording everyone coming and going. The ceremony and reception are not even near the crime scene. As of right now, it's probably the safest place they could be."

Sarah frowned as she looked at Mitchell. "The safest place they could be? With a murderer on the loose?"

"It seems to me that whoever did this had some kind of motive," Vicky said in an attempt to soothe her sister. "I don't think they're just going to go around causing more harm."

"I've gathered a few of the security guards in the banquet hall to interview them," Mitchell added, hoping to distract Sarah from her frustration. "I'm sure we'll have this cleared up soon."

While Mitchell interviewed the security guards, Vicky had a strong hunch. Yes, the pictures were of Trinie, which both Seth and Trinie would be hurt by if they came out into the public view, but they were not the only ones that could be hurt by such a thing. She recalled the argument that Aunt Ida had witnessed in the hallway outside Seth and Trinie's room. It was with Matt. Matt had been working with the couple for some time, and seemed to be appreciated by them. She remembered the rumor that Emily had told her about Matt having some drama in his past with the country singer, Charlotte. It seemed awfully coincidental to Vicky that Matt would be involved in two scandalous events, but maybe she was underestimating the amount of scandal and scrutiny that celebrities endured.

Vicky saw Aunt Ida walk into the lobby. She wanted to see if she knew anything about the photos of Charlotte that Emily had mentioned. After all Aunt Ida loved celebrities and gossip. "Aunt Ida!" Vicky called

"Hi," Aunt Ida replied with a large grin on her face as she walked towards her.

"I wanted to ask you something. Emily mentioned a scandal that involved photos of Charlotte, the country singer, and Seth's bodyguard, Matt Castille. I was wondering if you know anything about it?" Vicky questioned in a hushed voice.

"No, but we have to find out about it," Aunt Ida said with a sheepish grin. "Why don't you go surfing?"

"Do you mean look on the internet?" Vicky giggled.

"Yes. But I have to get ready for the wedding now," Aunt Ida said with anticipation. "I have to look my best," she smiled.

"Okay, I'll let you know what I find," Vicky whispered.

"Brilliant," Aunt Ida said with a flurry of her arms as she walked towards the stairs.

Vicky thought she might as well see what she could find out about Matt's debacle with Charlotte straight away. What harm could it do? Vicky went into Sarah's office while she was outside checking over everything for the wedding. Once inside, Vicky sat down at her sister's computer and began searching for information about Charlotte and Matt. Eventually, she came upon a very detailed article accompanied by a video. The article described an altercation between Charlotte and her long time bodyguard, Matt Castille. The singer had accused him of being the one who had provided a photographer the opportunity to snap pictures of her in the middle of a tryst with another singer's husband. Matt vehemently denied the accusations, but Charlotte was convinced he had made a deal with the photographer.

The entire argument culminated in a confrontation in the middle of the street in front of the singer's exclusive New York City apartment, which onlookers were only too happy to record. Vicky narrowed her eyes as she watched the video. The amount of expletives the young woman was using towards Matt was quite surprising, and very colorful at times. If Matt was connected to the photographer then maybe he was looking for the same kind of payday from working with Seth and Trinie. Her suspicions were confirmed when she read that the photographer in the middle of the scandal was none other than Graham Walker. He ended up exonerated and Matt was terminated from his job.

Vicky sat back in her chair and studied the screen as she watched the video once more. Matt looked absolutely horrified with the way Charlotte was speaking to him, and even appeared to have tears in his eyes as he looked away from her. He didn't look like someone who was trying to score an extra buck or two off the vulnerability of a young woman. Was it possible that he was that skilled an actor? It was hard for Vicky to put together the exact scenario that would lead to the same bodyguard and the same photographer being put into a similar position. The photographs were on Graham's computer, which would indicate that he had taken them. He was likely intending to blackmail the couple with them. But, was Matt involved? And if so, had a squabble over payment led to Graham's death?

"Vicky?" Aunt Ida's shrill voice called out from outside the office. "Are you in there?" she pushed the door open to discover Vicky sitting in front of Sarah's computer, her eyes wide, and one finger thoughtfully tapping the computer table.

"Don't you know what time it is?" Aunt Ida gasped as she rushed to Vicky's side.

"What time is it?" she asked with a slight frown of distraction. She was trying to piece everything together in her mind. "Is this important?"

"I don't know, is the wedding starting without you important?" she asked with a frown and waved one hand in front of Vicky's face. "Are you in there?"

"The wedding's starting?" Vicky asked as she jumped up out of the computer chair. "Oh no," she glanced at her watch. "I lost track of time. I've got to check on the musicians," she ran out of the office with Aunt Ida following right behind her. With everything that had been happening at the inn she had to wonder if it would be possible for the wedding to be successful. But there was no more time to wonder. She had only one choice, and that was to do the best job she could to make sure that Seth and Trinie had the best wedding that they possibly could. Even if there was a killer in their midst.

One thing was certain, Graham had those pictures with the intention of blackmailing the couple and extorting as much money out of them as possible. Was there someone else who had the pictures as well? As she hurried to the garden to check on the musicians, she heard the press shouting from outside the gates. As important as it was for her to find out who was behind the death of the photographer, the chaos of the beginning of the wedding was an unavoidable distraction. She had to check on the seating, the music, the priest, the list was endless. The entire time in the back of her mind she knew that someone she was talking to, smiling at, or reassuring might be the person behind this horrible crime. There was one person in particular that she was looking out for. She surveyed all the faces of the security guards she saw. But Matt was nowhere to be found.

"Have you seen your partner?" she asked Seth's other bodyguard as the groom was headed for the altar.

"No, haven't seen him, he must be with Trinie," the man said with a shrug and hurried after the man he was supposed to be protecting. Vicky frowned and headed for the bridal suite where Trinie was being prepared by several friends and family members. Trinie's mother had passed a few years before, so she had plenty of women around her to support her during the wedding. Matt was not blended among them, nor was he standing outside the bridal suite. Vicky wanted to figure out where he was but the ceremony was moving forward whether she was ready for it or not. Surprisingly, it was going very smoothly, and Trinie stole a moment to grab Vicky.

"Thank you so much," she said with gratitude before she was whisked out of the bridal suite. Aunt Ida had already found her seat and was eagerly observing the ceremony. She had her lavender scarf wrapped around her purple hair and was perched at the edge of her seat, just waiting for the bride to make her entrance. Vicky scanned the crowd again hoping to spot Matt, but once more he was missing. His absence sealed it once and for all in her mind. Wherever he was, he was hiding from something, as he certainly wasn't doing his job of protecting the bride. As she sat down near the back, she felt someone else sit down next to her. She glanced up with surprise to discover Mitchell settling into the chair right beside her.

"Mitchell," she exclaimed as she grabbed his hand. "I think I know who was behind the photographer's death," she blurted out. A few of the people seated around her glanced nervously in her direction, but the shift of the music from peaceful to the triumphant bridal march drew their attention away from anything that Vicky had to say.

"Shh," Mitchell said as he gave her hand a gentle squeeze in return. "This is my favorite part," he sighed and stood up with the rest of the guests as the flower girl emerged from behind the silk curtains that Vicky had set up to make the entrance even more dramatic. Their color matched the pale silver shade of the groom's tuxedo perfectly and made the bride's pure white gown stand out exquisitely. She sighed a little, surprising herself, as she watched Trinie emerge from the curtains behind her bridesmaids. She was carrying a bouquet of simple, small, pink roses, and the color splash was vibrant against her deeply tanned skin. She couldn't be more beautiful, Vicky was sure of it. When she felt Mitchell's arm curve around her waist she closed her eyes briefly. She tried to picture herself as the bride, walking down the aisle towards Mitchell, waiting for her. Her body stiffened, and Mitchell held her just a little tighter.

The very idea of being in a wedding dress made Vicky want to turn tail and run, but Trinie wasn't running. She was walking in perfect rhythm with the music, towards the man she adored. It was clear in her wide, almond gaze and the flush of her cheeks that she was in this for real, not for the press. Seth who waited for her at the altar looked as if he might want to run down the aisle towards her, but he restrained himself, vacillating between a stunned smile and an overjoyed grin as she approached. Vicky was moved by the strong emotion between the two, and so very grateful that the wedding had not been stalled by the crime that had taken place.

There was nothing more precious than the moment Seth extended his hand to her, and she laid hers against his palm. It was truly breathtaking, and she heard Mitchell take a sharp breath as he witnessed the same beauty that she did. When they sat back down in their chairs, he refused to release her hand, his eyes fixated on the ceremony that was taking place.

Chapter Seven

The office was empty, the door left partially open. Sarah had specifically stated in her discussion with the security guards that the door should always be locked if no one was in there. She insisted that the office remained locked all of the time because it contained the safe, as well as personal information about frequent customers, and her own personal information. So, when Matt saw the door standing slightly open he suspected something might be wrong. He was determined not to fail the celebrity couple he had been called to shield, as he cared about them and did not want his career to be ruined again. When he pushed the door slowly open he quickly assessed that the office was empty. But he needed to see if there was anything taken, or if perhaps someone had left a device of some kind set to disrupt the wedding that was taking place.

Matt noticed right away that the computer screen was lit up as if someone had been there recently. He walked over to it and sat down in front of the screen. On it he recognized the image of an angry Charlotte frozen in time by the video that was not playing. Tentatively, he slid the mouse over to point at the play button on the video, and it came to life. Matt knew what the video was about as soon as he heard Charlotte cursing and shrieking. He would never forget the accusations she had flung at him. He had been so stunned by her certainty that he was guilty. It still hurt him to recall it. Perhaps he had allowed himself to become too close to Charlotte. He had learned his lesson from that.

As the video played Matt's mind processed what he was seeing. Someone else had recently been in here, watching this video. Someone else had been looking into his encounter with Charlotte, and had probably read the attached article detailing the accusations by Graham that he had been involved. The same photographer who had been found dead. In that moment he knew that someone was onto him. But who? He didn't have to wait long for the answer, because he heard voices outside the office door.

"It was such a lovely ceremony," Aunt Ida declared as they neared the office.

"Yes it was," Vicky agreed, trying not to think too much about the silent interaction that had occurred between herself and Mitchell.

She had to stay focused on what she had discovered about the bodyguard. She had been watching for him during the entire ceremony, but had not spotted him. This worried her as she wondered if he was going to seek revenge on anyone else. From what she had seen in the video she could assume that he had only wanted to attack the photographer, but she didn't know that for sure. Maybe after his encounter with Charlotte he had found himself so angry at celebrities that he wanted to take it out on the newly married couple.

"I really don't want to miss the reception," Aunt Ida lamented as she kept her pace as even as she could. The high heeled shoes she wore were much higher than she was used to, which made it rather difficult to walk.

"I don't either," Vicky admitted. "We won't though. They are taking photographs with the guests first." She wanted to make sure that everything went smoothly. She couldn't let that distract her now though, she had to focus on figuring out what to do about the bodyguard. Mitchell had been abruptly whisked away by the sheriff after the ceremony so she couldn't tell him about Matt.

"Wait until you see this," Vicky added as she pushed the door to the office open. She quietly chastised herself for leaving it open, and hoped that Sarah hadn't noticed. If she had the door would have likely been closed and locked, so she was fairly certain that she had escaped her sister's wrath on this particular issue. When she stepped inside she was stunned to discover the hulking presence sitting in front of the computer. At first she was too surprised to react, but he wasn't. He must have heard them coming because he was already standing up from the desk chair.

"Uh, what are you doing in here?" Vicky stammered out, she hoped that he didn't realize that she suspected him. But the video was still playing on the screen.

"You just couldn't leave it alone, could you?" he asked her in a cruel voice as he began to advance on her.

"I don't know what you mean..." she started to say but fell silent as he reached for the gun on his hip. Aunt Ida gasped from behind her. Vicky could see the cold rage in the man's eyes that indicated he would do whatever it took to make sure that they never saw the light of day again.

"Aunt Ida," she hissed as she grabbed her aunt's hand. "Run!" They went into the hallway and no one was around because they were still taking photos of the guests and the staff were setting up the reception. Aunt Ida was running as fast as she could but she was teetering on those expensive high heels and cursing herself for not finding that extra half-inch in her shoe size to be that important. She felt as if her toes were going to burst in the tip of her shoes as she ran beside Vicky. Matt took a few seconds to follow because he closed down the webpage.

"Keep going, keep going," Vicky was chanting as she steered her aunt passed a row of rolling carts in the hallway. Vicky pushed them into the way to try to block Matt who was fast approaching. But a moment later she heard the man's boots, close behind, striking the floor once more. They were headed as quickly as they could for the kitchen.

"Stop!" he bellowed after them. "Stop where you are!"

Vicky took a sharp breath, knowing that the man was armed. All of the security guards were carrying weapons and she knew for a fact that they were loaded.

"Don't slow down," Vicky pleaded with her aunt as she practically dragged her around the corner of the hallway. What if they shouted for help and Matt opened fire? Who knew how many innocent bystanders he would shoot. No, they just needed to get somewhere safe, that was the main goal in Vicky's mind. They had to get somewhere that they could block him out. When they ran towards the kitchen and she saw the door to the wine cellar standing half open, she knew that it was the perfect place. She pulled her aunt towards the cellar door. The wine cellar was the best option. As soon as they stepped through the door, Vicky tried to shove it closed and lock it behind her. Aunt Ida stumbled down the stairs, hanging onto the railing as she did. As Vicky was just about to lock the door, the full force of the massive security guard slammed against it.

"Open the door!" he shouted. Vicky struggled to shove back, but she was no match for his size or strength, and she found her feet sliding back across the top step of the wooden stairs that led down into the wine cellar. He forced the door all the way open, causing Vicky to stumble on the steps. She slid down them and landed hard on her back. The cement floor was harsh along her spine and she groaned in pain. As she forced herself to open her eyes and look up the stairs she met the barrel of a gun which was being pointed directly down at her. Matt had shut and locked the door behind him, and was standing two steps above her with the weapon promising to solve the problem within a split second.

"No, don't," Ida demanded as she came to Vicky's side.

"Stay back," Vicky shouted to her aunt, as she struggled not to move a muscle.

"Shut up, both of you," the bodyguard barked and released the safety catch on his weapon. "It seems we have a little problem."

"It doesn't have to be a problem," Vicky assured him, ignoring his command for silence. Her back was screaming in pain from striking the floor but she tried to remain still. "Look, you killed the photographer in a fit of rage," Vicky explained to him calmly. "He was trying to ruin your life, again. It's okay, a jury will understand that," she assured him. "But coldly gunning down two innocent women in a basement, that's not something they'll forgive," Vicky insisted, glaring at him. "So, just let us go," she pleaded as she looked up at the man. "Let us go, and we'll settle all of this."

"Or," the bodyguard laughed as if he had been entertained by her entire speech. "I'll just take you out to that nice big lake that's only a few miles away, and dump your bodies. No bodies, no crime, and no one to stick their noses into my business!" he announced and descended the last two steps.

Aunt Ida stood her ground. Vicky shifted on the floor in pain.

"You see," he murmured as he looked from Vicky to Ida, and then back to Vicky again. "I've been in this line of work a long time. I know how to make people just disappear. So the two of you, well, you'll be missed. But I doubt they'll look too hard. No children, no husbands." he chuckled at that and cast a light wink in their direction.

"You're a terrible man," Aunt Ida abruptly announced as she stared up at him. She had never seen someone so vicious before.

"Maybe," he shrugged and offered a mild sigh. "But maybe that's because I've seen where being a good person gets you, darling. It gets you accused of things you never did. It gets you bankruptcy, a lost house, a lost career. I never had anything to do with those pictures. Not with Charlotte and not with Trinie. It was all Graham and he made millions off the sale of the photographs. When he told me he had some of Trinie I just snapped. I got so angry that I just wanted it to stop, the invasion of privacy, the harassment. I wanted him to experience the consequences of his actions. So, that's where being a good person gets you. It gets you locked in a wine cellar, counting down the minutes to when I will come back for you."

"Give me your phones," he demanded. Vicky and Aunt Ida reluctantly handed over their cell phones with trembling hands.

With that he backed up the stairs, keeping the gun trained on the two of them.

"You make a move on me, I'll shoot you both right now," he warned them. Then he rested his hand on the locked door. "At least this way, you'll have the chance to say your goodbyes."

Vicky reached out to gently grasp her aunt's hand. She wanted to attack the man, but she knew that whatever she could do would be no match for the weapon he held. As he closed the door behind him, she heard the bolt slide into place on the outside of the door. She sighed and closed her eyes as she felt Aunt Ida's arms encircle her.

"Don't you worry, Vicky," she whispered to her. "We've been in much tougher spots than this before, haven't we?"

Vicky nodded a little, but she was not convinced. She felt as if they were stuck with no way out. The two sat there for a few moments, savoring each other's comfort, before Ida bravely spoke up.

"Well, we're not going to escape by snuggling," she said flatly and stood up from the floor. Vicky stood up too, wincing from the pain in her back, and they began to inspect their surroundings. Though Vicky had been in the wine cellar plenty of times before, she had never looked at it quite in this way. She had never needed to find an escape from it before. Aunt Ida cautiously climbed the stairs to test the door.

"Oh dear, we're not getting out of here," Vicky announced after Aunt Ida rattled the knob a few times. The lock was solid and there was no chance of getting it open.

"Don't be ridiculous Vicky, I can take him down, we'll get out of here," Aunt Ida announced with confidence.

"Maybe we can find something to pry it open," Vicky said as she glanced around the cellar. Unfortunately, all she saw were racks and racks of wine bottles.

Ida slowly walked back down the small set of wooden steps to reach the cement floor. "What do you think he will do when he comes back? If we have an idea we can be prepared."

Vicky sighed as she glanced up at the ceiling. She wondered if she could make enough noise banging on it to get someone's attention. But with all the wedding festivities she doubted anyone would hear it.

"I agree. I think," Vicky said slowly as she looked back at her aunt, "that we need to be ready for him when he comes back." She frowned as she crouched down and peered at the ribbon of light that was pouring in from beneath the door. She knew that would be their only warning, when his large boots blocked the light. Then they would know that he had returned.

"How?" Ida began to walk the length of the cellar thinking of what she could use.

"We just have to use being stuck in this cellar to our advantage," Vicky said sternly. She didn't want to die in the cellar. She kept Mitchell in the forefront of her mind. There was too much yet unspoken for it all to end this way.

With renewed determination Vicky looked around at the wine that surrounded them. It was just about the only thing they had in the cellar to use in their defense. She picked up a wine bottle and gave it a swift test swing. She could swing it hard, but would it be hard enough? She looked up the stairs and realized that when he opened the door he would be able to see her coming. There was nowhere to hide behind the door and jump out behind him as the steps lead right up to the door. She grimaced and was just about to lay the bottle of wine back on the shelf, when she struck her hand on the wooden corner of it. Her hand jerked and the bottle slipped from her fingers.

The bottle splattered against the floor. Drops of wine and tiny shreds of glass spread across the cellar in all directions. The bulk of the wine spilled right at the base of the stairs.

"Vicky, are you okay?" Ida asked and started to rush to her side.

"Wait, Aunt Ida," Vicky called out sharply. "Be careful or you'll slip!"

Aunt Ida stopped before the puddle and her eyes met Vicky's as they both realized a solution to their problem.

"That's it!" Vicky announced, her eyes widening with excitement. "We just have to make a puddle for him to slip in! If we can get him down, then we can surely keep him down!"

Ida was smiling at her niece's words, as if she had had the same idea.

"Sounds like a great plan to me," she agreed.

"Well, it's the only one we have," Vicky pointed out and winced as she felt a bolt of pain run through her arm. She looked down at her left forearm to discover a small gash. One of the pieces of glass must have cut her as it sprung upward from the floor.

"Vicky, you're bleeding," Ida said with concern and carefully stepped across the puddle of wine. She looked closely at the wound on Vicky's arm.

"It's okay," Vicky assured her. "It's just a little cut."

"Hmm, and the grand canyon is just a little ditch," Aunt Ida murmured. Then she untangled the long lavender scarf she had tied around her hair. "Here," she said as she began to wind it around Vicky's arm.

"But Aunt Ida you love that scarf," Vicky pointed out and started to draw her arm back.

"Silly girl," Ida chuckled and gripped Vicky's wrist firmly, so that she could hold her arm still as she wrapped the scarf around it. "I don't love things, I love people, namely yourself and your sister and her family. Nothing else has any real value," she smiled with pride as she wrapped the scarf tightly to help stop the flow of blood. Vicky stared at her with admiration. It had been troubling her to think that Aunt Ida might have given up so much in order to step in and help care for her nieces. In that moment she saw the truth in her aunt's eyes. Being there for them had never been a burden. Vicky sighed with relief and picked up a bottle of wine.

"Well, if we're going to spill some, we might as well drink some," she suggested and snatched two wine glasses from where they were placed on a low shelf hanging from the ceiling. She handed one to her aunt and poured a glass for herself as well.

"To family," Aunt Ida said as she held up her glass of wine.

"To overcoming adversity," Vicky said with a wink as they clinked their glasses together. The two downed their wine rather quickly, as if they were having a little bit of a race. Ida won, and set her glass down on the floor beside her.

"About that adversity," Ida pointed her finger towards the door. "I have a feeling it's not going to be long before he comes back."

"I think you're right," Vicky nodded, her head swimming a little from guzzling her wine. "He's probably going to use the noise of the party as cover, so we'll need to make sure that we're ready for him."

The two women began opening and pouring bottles of wine all over the floor. As the crimson liquid splashed against the cement Vicky could only hope that this would work.

Chapter Eight

It wasn't long before the boots on the other side of the door fell heavily against the wooden floor.

"This is it," Vicky told her aunt as she motioned for the woman to hide behind one of the shelves of wine. "I'm going to distract him the best I can," she whispered to Aunt Ida. "You be ready with a bottle of wine, just in case, okay?"

"Here we go!" Aunt Ida nodded and grabbed one of the biggest bottles of wine she could find. She crouched behind the shelf as they heard the door slowly open. In the same moment that the door swung open, Vicky swung a bottle of wine up at the light bulb, breaking it, and plunging the cellar into almost complete darkness. She knew it was a risk, as it would make it harder to attack him, but it would also reduce the chance of him seeing the puddle of wine.

"What was that?" he snarled, pushing the door and only partially closing it behind him. He whipped out a small penlight that was attached to his belt along with his weapon and a club.

Vicky cringed inwardly as she hadn't thought about the flashlight. Luckily, he flicked it around the wine cellar shelves and not the floor.

"Ow, I'm hurt," Vicky called out. "Oh please help me," she whined from the bottom of the stairs. Just as she had hoped, he moved swiftly down the stairs, so swiftly that when he set his heavy boot in the puddle of wine it slipped right up out from under him and his entire body flew up into the air. His head came down first, cracking on the bottom step.

Vicky jumped up at the same moment that Aunt Ida rounded the side of the shelf. Aunt Ida had her bottle of wine poised and ready to go and so did Vicky. But as they stood over the large man, they discovered that he was not moving. The light from the still open doorway of the cellar revealed that his eyes were closed.

"He must have been knocked out by the fall," Vicky murmured cautiously. She still hesitated to move too close.

"The big ones always fall the hardest," Aunt Ida said as she looked down at the man.

"Help!" Vicky shouted up the stairs to the open door. She didn't want to risk climbing over the man. "Help us!" she shrieked.

"Please, let me," Aunt Ida cleared her throat. The scream that poured from between the woman's perfectly painted lips was akin to the most professionally trained opera singer. Vicky had to reach up to cover her ears in an attempt to block it out. As she closed her eyes and ducked her head, she almost overlooked the man stirring on the floor before them. As soon as the movement registered in her mind Vicky's eyes sprung back open. The man was starting to sit up.

"Aunt Ida?" she heard Sarah calling from the kitchen. "Aunt Ida is that you?"

"Aunt Ida, he's awake!" Vicky declared as the bodyguard reached for his weapon and began to draw it. Aunt Ida and Vicky each slammed the bottle of wine in their hands down hard against the side of his head. They aimed for the temple. The crack of glass against skin, and then the burst of the bottles shattering, drowned out Mitchell's calls from the top of the stairs. When Vicky and Aunt Ida looked up at him he had his gun drawn and was staring at them in amazement as the large man slumped back down to the floor.

"Get back," he shouted at them and hurried down the steps.

"Be careful!" Vicky cried out, as she didn't want him to slip. Vicky and Aunt Ida stepped back a few paces as Mitchell disarmed the bodyguard.

Sarah was standing at the top of the stairs, one hand covering her mouth, her eyes spread wide. "Are you okay?" she called out to them. Mitchell was on his radio calling for medics as well as back up and reporting the crime that had taken place.

"Sure, want some wine?" Aunt Ida offered as she held up a bottle of wine.

"No," Sarah said incredulously as she stared down at her sister and her aunt and slowly shook her head. "How do the two of you get into these messes?"

Vicky smiled happily at her aunt, who only shrugged innocently.

"Just lucky I guess," Aunt Ida smiled. Vicky could not believe how calm she looked. She reached out her hand and felt her silky skin settle against her palm. Mitchell slid the knocked-out man away from the stairs so that they could go up to Sarah. When Sarah saw the blood leaking through the scarf tied around Vicky's arm, she gasped.

"Oh no, you're hurt," she tugged Vicky towards the large sink in the kitchen.

"It's fine, really," she tried to assure her sister, but Sarah would not let go of her wrists.

Tears filled Sarah's eyes as she stared down at the cut she had unwrapped.

"Sarah it's okay," Vicky said gently. "I'm okay, and everything is fine now," she murmured reassuringly while clutching her back. When Vicky looked up she could see the deep fear in Sarah's eyes.

"Vicky, what would I ever do without you?" Sarah asked with panic in her voice. "Do you even know how important you are to me?"

"I'm sure you'd manage just fine, Sarah," Vicky said in a clipped voice as she struggled to control her emotions.

"No Vicky," Sarah murmured and held her sister's gaze with her own. "I would never manage without you. Please, you have to be more careful," she insisted as the medics arrived and took over the care of Vicky's arm.

"I will be," Vicky promised her. As Mitchell entered the kitchen he met Vicky's gaze with the same fear in his eyes.

"Now exactly what happened here?" the sheriff demanded as he walked into the kitchen before Vicky and Mitchell had a chance to speak.

Mitchell looked as if he was ready to point out how Vicky and Aunt Ida had gotten into the middle of the investigation, but as he studied the man, he lowered his head slightly.

"Well, Sheriff, turns out, there was a bit more going on behind the scenes. I'll fill you in," he said respectfully. He steered him down the steps to take in the crime scene. As Mitchell walked down the stairs he glanced back over his shoulder to look at Vicky. A small smile played across his lips as he met her eyes. It was all she needed to see to know exactly what he meant. The love between them was blossoming, even if yet unspoken. When he did speak, it was with a playful tone, "don't forget about that vacation!"

The End

More Cozy Mysteries by Cindy Bell

Bekki the Beautician Cozy Mysteries

Hairspray and Homicide

A Dyed Blonde and a Dead Body

Mascara and Murder

Pageant and Poison

Heavenly Highland Inn Cozy Mysteries

Murdering the Roses